Tears Streamed Down Casey's Cheeks. "Just Let Me Go . . . _please_."

"I can't do that. I can't _ever_ do that."

Michael pulled her into his arms and held her trembling body with infinite gentleness.

They stood silhouetted against the bonfire, a man and a woman embracing.

From the terrace, Richard looked out onto the lawn and saw them. He knew immediately who it was. Yet in his mind's eye the two figures darkly silhouetted against the blazing fire took on a different shape. The other people strolling on the lawn faded from sight, as did the terrace, the mansion, the sounds of partying coming from within. The brisk October evening became a bitterly cold night in late winter. And the figures silhouetted against the fire were he and Jesse . . .

Dear Reader:

Nora Roberts, Tracy Sinclair, Jeanne Stephens, Carole Halston, Linda Howard. Are these authors familiar to you? We hope so, because they are just a few of our most popular authors who publish with Silhouette Special Edition each and every month. And the Special Edition list is changing to include new writers with fresh stories. It has been said that discovering a new author is like making a new friend. So during these next few months, be sure to look for books by Sandi Shane, Dorothy Glenn and other authors who have just written their first and second Special Editions, stories we hope you enjoy.

Choosing which Special Editions to publish each month is a pleasurable task, but not an easy one. We look for stories that are sophisticated, sensuous, touching, and great love stories, as well. These are the elements that make Silhouette Special Editions more romantic...and unique.

So we hope you'll find this Silhouette Special Edition just that—*Special*—and that the story finds a special place in your heart.

The Editors at Silhouette

SERL-7/85

PAMELA WALLACE
Tears in the Rain

Silhouette Special Edition
Published by Silhouette Books New York
America's Publisher of Contemporary Romance

To my big, handsome brothers, Timothy
Bianco and Dennis Bradley, with love.

SILHOUETTE BOOKS
300 E. 42nd St., New York, N.Y. 10017

Copyright © 1985 by Pamela Wallace

Distributed by Pocket Books

ISBN: 0-373-09255-5

First Silhouette Books printing August, 1985

10 9 8 7 6 5 4 3 2 1

America's Publisher of Contemporary Romance

Printed in the U.S.A.
BC91

PAMELA WALLACE

is a professional writer who has written for TV and magazines, as well as numerous works of fiction. Her spirited characters come alive on every page as she weaves a thought-provoking story of true-to-life romance. Ms Wallace lives in Fresno, California.

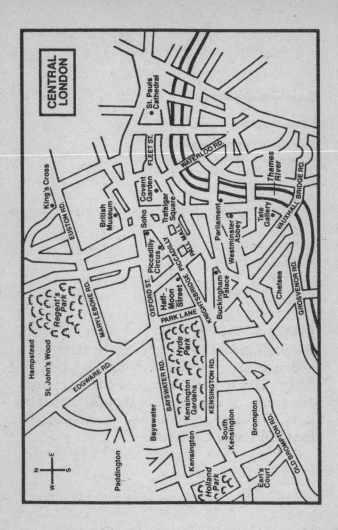

Prologue
London, 1944

It was a time when evil and good were clearly defined, a time when courage and honor weren't just empty words. Death was a constant possibility and therefore life was more precious. Amidst the sacrifice and destruction, passion ran deep. Because there wasn't time to waste, the moment had to be seized.

In London, against a litany of sirens, bombs and death, a man and a woman caught up in that turbulent time met and fell in love. That love forever changed both them and the generation that followed. . . .

Piccadilly Circus was crowded as usual with Londoners and Yank and British soldiers. A young RAF lieutenant made his way through the people lined up to board red double-decker buses. He was tall and lean, with classic Anglo-Saxon good looks—flaxen hair, slate-blue eyes and a strong face.

An aquiline nose and strong chin hinted at generations of well-bred ancestors. But there was humor in the full, passionate mouth and his entire demeanor had an engaging cockiness that implied he didn't take himself too seriously. Only the carefully veiled expression in those soft blue eyes suggested that he'd seen far too much in his twenty-three years.

He was in uniform, as were many of the men and women waiting to board the buses. Like them, he wore his uniform comfortably, as if it were a second skin. He'd had a while to get used to it. England had been at war for a long time.

From a nearby music shop came the sound of a phonograph playing "I'll Be Seeing You." The young flight lieutenant smiled to himself and for an instant his face was almost boyish. There was a certain someone he'd be seeing soon.

Oh, God, he could hardly wait to hold her in his arms again. The hours they spent together were so few, and even sweeter because of that. Each time he flew a mission, he knew that some men wouldn't return, and maybe, this time, *he* would be one of the unlucky ones. Sometimes, when it was especially bad, he almost hoped he would be unlucky, just to get the damn thing over with.

Then he thought the only reason to live was to see her again—to feel the incredible softness of her, to forget fear and death by losing himself in her.

It began to drizzle. He pulled up the collar of his leather flight jacket and smiled wryly. April in England. Nothing like the warm, beautiful springs where she came from, she had told him the last time they were together in the rain.

"You Yanks think everything about your country's better," he'd teased.

"Not everything," she'd answered, looking up at him with those incredible golden eyes in a way that had made him want to take her in his arms and keep her there forever.

The rain grew heavier. He shoved his hands deep in the pockets of his jacket and glanced around. Posters on the walls proclaimed, "Better Pot Luck with Churchill Today Than Humble Pie with Hitler Tomorrow. Don't Waste Food." And, "After Duty —15 Minutes' Pleasure and Satisfaction with a Churchman's No. 1 Cigarette."

As if a leisurely smoke could erase the memory of flying in heavy flak in the dark of night, dropping bombs, killing God knew how many people, women and children among them. And watching planes right next to him go down, carrying his friends to their deaths. And every one of them so young . . . so damn young.

There were times in the middle of the insanity of a world at war when he thought the only thing that made any sense was lying with her, feeling her short, slender body pressed against his, knowing that he stilled her fear as she stilled his.

He quickened his pace as he reached Half-Moon Street. The need to see her was urgent now.

Then he was at Half-Moon Square, the tiny park that was their meeting place. His body relaxed slightly. Soon she would be there. And in a matter of minutes, or hours, depending on how much time each had, they would lie together and make the war go away—for a little while.

As he stood in the rain at the edge of the park, his

fingers played with the small, foil-wrapped package in his pocket. She'd be surprised when he gave her a gift. They'd known each other such a short while, there'd been no time for presents.

Except one. A locket that had belonged to his mother, which he kept with him for luck. It was gold and round and embossed with his family crest—two lions rising up against each other ferociously. She hadn't wanted to accept such a valuable gift, but he'd insisted.

"You're my luck now," he'd told her.

Now, he thought that she'd be even more surprised when she opened this present. She didn't trust his love for her. She never actually admitted it, but it was obvious in the transparent relief that lit her face each time he showed up at the square.

Well, he thought happily, a wide gold wedding band should convince her how much she meant to him. In his other pocket was a special license. They could be married immediately. She might argue, as she had done when they'd first met, that they were too different, were worlds apart. It didn't matter. All that mattered was how perfectly their hearts and minds and bodies meshed.

He watched the faces of the people hurrying past, searching for one particular face. Heart-shaped. Pale. Lovely. Once, a girl in a tan trench coat, with long red hair hanging wetly past her shoulders, went by. He almost called out to her before he realized she wasn't Jesse.

The rain came down harder and he moved under a tree.

By evening there were fewer people and the small

square was nearly deserted. Still, the young soldier waited. She *had* to come. She always did, and tonight, of all nights, couldn't be any different.

Long past midnight, a passing policeman urged him to go in out of the rain. Without saying a word to the concerned policeman, he turned and walked away.

Jesse hadn't come. . . .

Chapter One

*C*asey Cantrell pulled the collar of her tan trench coat up around her face and dashed madly through the drizzle. Raindrops plopped softly on her cheeks, coursed over the freckles on her short, upturned nose and beaded her golden-brown lashes. When she opened her wide, full mouth slightly, she caught a hint of the natural taste of rainwater on the tip of her tongue.

Casey's face had always been rather babyish. It had been the bane of her existence when she was younger and longed to look sophisticated rather than innocent. The fact that she was petite, only five feet two inches tall and barely a hundred pounds soaking wet, hadn't helped.

But now, at twenty-eight, she was finally gaining a more mature beauty. Her cheeks were no longer quite so full: the bone structure she had yearned for and almost despaired of had emerged at last. And the lush mouth that had once seemed almost pouty had acquired a womanly sensuality.

Her long hair, made curly by the dampness, flew behind her in wet tendrils. It was red, but not the usual brash carroty color or more subtle auburn. Instead it was bronze, the rich, deep shade of a slightly used penny.

Silently, Casey cursed the sudden storm, the packed sidewalks of London and the maddeningly deliberate English. They weren't about to let a little rain hurry them in any way. Everything seemed to conspire to keep her from reaching her destination.

Growing wetter and more impatient by the minute, Casey finally threw caution to the wind. Leaving the pavement, she wound through two lanes of black taxis, tiny minis and a gleaming gray Bentley sedan that were stopped at a signal. Then she cut across Half-Moon Square, a tiny oasis of grass, flowers and trees surrounded by a black wrought-iron fence.

But Casey was oblivious to the quaint beauty of the tiny square. All she could think of was getting to the office building on the far side of it—and finally meeting the person who'd dominated her thoughts for the past week.

She was also oblivious to the Bentley. When the traffic light changed, it had gone around the square, then stopped in front of the building where Casey was heading. Inside the car, a middle-aged man stared at her. He was impeccably dressed in a wool-lined Burberry and held a tightly wound black umbrella and homburg.

With an odd, startled expression on his face, he watched as she made her way through puddles and around the few remaining late-blooming flowers, passing under the plane trees that were scant protection from the now heavy rain.

The chauffeur got out and opened the door as usual. When the man inside didn't move, the chauffeur bent down slightly to look inside. "Are you all right, my lord?"

Lord Richard Bredon came to with a start. "Yes . . . of course."

Getting out of the car, he hurried into the building.

As the chauffeur got back into the car, he muttered curiously, "Looked like he'd seen a ghost, he did."

Two minutes later, Casey walked through the stained-glass doors of Bredon Enterprises. The reception room was large and quietly impressive. Everything about it, from the plush green carpet to the antique furniture, from the fire blazing cheerfully in the marble-manteled fireplace to the old, gilt-framed paintings on the walls, spoke quietly but forcefully of money. Old money. And lots of it.

Whatever Casey had expected, somehow it wasn't this. All she'd known of Richard Bredon was a name on a fading envelope. Her mind had been filled with questions about him, and her vivid imagination had conjured up all sorts of images. But not this.

She felt her courage, which had been on shaky ground already, ebb.

"May I help you, miss?"

Turning around, Casey came face to face with an older woman, probably in her late fifties, immaculately and conservatively attired in a gray tweed suit. Her long, pale pink nails looked as if they'd never typed a letter. The receptionist, Casey decided.

Trying hard not to look as nervous and unsure as

she felt, she said firmly, "Yes, I'd like to see Mr. Bredon, please."

The woman sat down behind a lovely rosewood desk in the corner and glanced at an appointment calendar. "Your name, please?"

"Casey Cantrell."

The woman frowned slightly. "I'm afraid I don't see your name here, Miss Cantrell."

This was going to be the hard part. Afraid of being rebuffed over the telephone, Casey had opted to simply show up and hope Bredon would agree to see her. She said now, "I don't have an appointment. I just arrived this morning from the United States and I need to see Mr. Bredon on urgent, personal business."

The woman gave her a quick, appraising look. It took in the worn raincoat hanging over one arm and dripping onto the expensive carpet, the cream-colored wool dress and matching pumps that were stylish but obviously not designer made. And finally, Casey herself.

Casey had heard that the English had trouble categorizing Americans according to class. But not this receptionist: with that one look she immediately —and accurately—classified Casey as "not quite *quite*." Pursing her lips, she said dismissively, "*Lord* Bredon never sees anyone without an appointment." Her voice, which had been merely clipped and impersonal at first, was now patently unfriendly.

Lord Bredon? Casey felt her confusion mount as her courage waned. But she'd made up her mind to fulfill her late mother's last request on this trip, and she wasn't going to be put off by a frosty, smugly superior receptionist.

Holding herself as erect as possible, she raised her

chin in that "the world be damned" attitude her friends knew so well. "I have a letter for Lord Bredon. It's extremely important."

"Then please give it to me and I will see that His Lordship gets it."

"No. I must deliver it personally to Lord Bredon himself."

That wasn't precisely true. Her instructions were simply to see that he got the letter. But she was too curious about the whole affair not to find out as much as possible about it.

The receptionist hesitated. This was clearly an unusual situation, one she wasn't entirely sure how to handle.

At that moment the intercom on the receptionist's desk buzzed. She answered it and after a moment said, "Yes, my lord. By the way, there is a young woman—an American—here to see you. She doesn't have an appointment. She *says* she has a letter to give you."

There was a long pause. Finally, the receptionist finished crisply, "Yes, my lord."

Putting down the receiver, she looked up at Casey with barely disguised surprise and curiosity. "His Lordship will see you. His office is through that door."

Casey felt a thousand butterflies take wing deep inside her as she walked through the door. Now, for the first time since finding the letter and the brief accompanying instructions, she would get to the bottom of the mystery.

The inner office was even larger and more impressive than the reception area. Here, too, was a fireplace with a briskly burning fire to ward off the chill of this early October morning. A magnificent

Oriental carpet covered most of the parquet floor, and floor-to-ceiling bookcases on two walls were filled with leather-bound volumes.

But Casey only took in these details out of the corner of her eye: her attention was focused on the man sitting behind a massive mahogany desk. He rose politely as she crossed the room.

He was tall and thin, with blond hair just beginning to turn silver and slate-blue eyes that appraised her coolly. His face was nearly unlined and attractive. Casey guessed his age to be around sixty. In his youth, she suspected, he'd been very handsome indeed. Now, by his bearing and manner, fitted in the elegance of a Savile Row suit and with a direct gaze that betrayed not a hint of indecision, he was almost venerable.

"How do you do, Miss . . ."

"Cantrell. Casey Cantrell."

When she took his extended hand, he let it drop almost immediately. Beneath his polished, polite façade, she sensed he was holding himself tightly in check. The slight trembling of his hand revealed that he wasn't as calm as he had at first appeared.

Why? Casey wondered.

They both sat down. Casey was far too nervous by now to do anything but come straight to the point.

"I have a letter for you."

"So I understand. May I ask why you didn't simply post it?"

"It's not my letter. I'm delivering it for someone else."

"I see. That still doesn't explain why you didn't give it to my receptionist to hand on to me."

"My instructions were to see that you got it."

"And you took those instructions literally?"

There was no amusement in his tone, only a growing irritation.

Casey had a nervous habit of fiddling with a necklace, a small gold pendant on a short chain, the only jewelry she normally wore. Now she pulled at the chain until the pendant came out from under the high neckline of her dress.

She was about to explain about the letter when she saw that Lord Bredon was staring at her pendant with an expression almost of shock.

"Where did you get that?" he demanded.

Taken aback at the sudden harshness in his voice, Casey stammered, "My—my mother gave it to me." Then, pulling herself together, she went on, "You see, the letter is from her. I found it among her things. It was in an envelope, and written on the envelope were the instructions to see that it was given to you."

His pale blue eyes went from the pendant to her face. "Who is your mother, young woman?"

"She was Jesse Cantrell."

There was a long pause, during which the room was utterly silent save for the soft crackle of wood burning in the fireplace.

Lord Bredon's voice was barely a whisper. "Was?"

"She died a month ago. I only got around to going through her personal papers last week and I found *this*." Taking an envelope from her purse, she laid it on the desk. It was old and faded and completely blank except for two words—Richard Bredon.

He stared at it as if it were alive and might actually move at any moment. A mask seemed to slip and what Casey saw beneath it astonished her. There was nothing imposing about him now.

Watching him, she couldn't believe the transformation he was undergoing. He'd been impersonal and businesslike at first. Now his face seemed to dissolve, to grow years older in an instant.

For some reason she didn't understand, she felt a twinge of pity for him.

"Have you read this letter?" he asked slowly.

"No. It's sealed. Obviously, it's private."

"Did your mother ever speak of me?"

"Never. I'll be perfectly frank, Lord Bredon. It's totally unlike my mother to do something like this. I'm naturally curious about the letter, and about what kind of relationship she could possibly have had with you. As far as I knew, she never left Kentucky. And you certainly never visited our farm there."

He'd been staring past her as she spoke. Now he made a visible effort to pull himself together. He met her look, and his expression was once more tightly controlled.

"You've made a long journey for nothing, Miss Cantrell. I don't know anything about your mother. And I have no wish to read any letter from her."

Casey was stunned—and angry. In that state, she wasn't given to mincing words. "That's a lie! Obviously you knew her."

"I'm not accustomed to having my word questioned, young woman." He rose and looked down at her. "Good day."

She stood and faced him. She hadn't gotten this far, and spent so much time wondering what on earth it was all about, just to be dismissed so peremptorily.

"Lord Bredon, this letter was written to you."

"Well, I don't want it." Picking it up, he held it

out to her. When she didn't take it, he shoved it into
her hand. "And I don't want to see or hear from you
again. I repeat, good day."

Turning abruptly, Casey strode out. She ignored
the pointed stare of the receptionist and slammed
the door behind her as she went out into the hall.
Humiliation washed over her. She'd been tossed out
on her ear, treated like some panhandler or worse.
She didn't understand Lord Bredon's rudeness.

No, she thought, it went beyond rudeness. He had
shown real anger and bitterness toward her.

As she stepped into the elevator, she smoothed
out the crumpled envelope with his name on it. Why
had he refused to even look at it? Wasn't he at least
curious about its contents?

She certainly was. More so than ever now. As she
stared at it, she was consumed with an intense desire
to open it and read it. The letter was very old.
Whatever words it contained had been written a long
time ago. Surely they couldn't be that important any
longer.

And yet . . . the envelope had been carefully
sealed, without even a tiny corner left open. Then it
had been placed in a larger envelope, along with the
brief instructions. Her mother clearly had intended
no one but Richard Bredon to read this letter.

Casey knew she couldn't break the trust implicit in
her mother's action. Reluctantly, she put the envelope in her purse.

In his office, Richard Bredon sat in his tall-backed
leather chair, lost in thought. Though he'd turned
his chair to face the window that overlooked Half-
Moon Square, he saw nothing of the bustle going on
two stories below.

For thirty-nine years he'd gotten through each day by rigidly refusing to look back at the past. If he could have erased all memory of the war, he would have. Barring that, he simply refused to talk or think about it.

Other men attended annual squadron reunions, made sentimental journeys to Normandy battle sites and exchanged forty-year-old anecdotes. Not he. He never discussed his involvement in the war. His medals and decorations were stored away in a box that hadn't been opened since he was demobilized.

Yet in an impulsive moment he'd bought this office building because it overlooked Half-Moon Square. He hadn't analyzed the irresistible push-pull of the location. He'd simply told himself it was a good deal financially.

Five days a week he came here. Often he looked out thoughtfully over the square that had changed so little in the intervening years. But even in the privacy of his own thoughts, he refused to conjure up images that were still all too painful.

Now a disturbing young woman had suddenly come into his life and brought the past with her. For a moment his iron self-control wavered and he allowed himself the bittersweet luxury of remembering. The face that for so long had betrayed no emotion beyond the most superficial now softened.

Finally he whispered one word:

"*Jesse.*"

The face that he'd spent so long trying to banish from his memory appeared as vividly as if he were looking at a photograph. Golden-brown eyes . . . bronze hair that fell in thick, soft waves past gently sloping shoulders . . . a tiny cleft in a round chin.

Leaning back in his chair, he closed his eyes and remembered the very first time he'd seen her. . . .

"Come on, Richard, I promised Jesse I'd be there."

"That's your dutiful tone, Emily. I remember it well. When you were ten, it meant we had to stop playing and go in to tea. And when you were fifteen, it meant I had to be polite and listen to your father's old war stories when I'd much rather be out riding with you."

Her deep blue eyes sparkled with humor. "Well, you *were* incorrigible." But as she looked at him, her expression sobered. "Are you tired? Was it . . . a bad mission?"

"There's no such thing as a good one." His tone was curt. Then, realizing he'd responded to her concern with rudeness, he said, "All right. I'll go meet your new flatmate. And afterwards we'll have champagne."

"Oh, good. That should cheer her up. Poor thing, she's had rather a rough time of it."

Who hasn't? he wondered bitterly. But he didn't say so.

He helped Emily into her coat, then slipped on his leather flight jacket. After four years it was beginning to seem like the only jacket he'd ever worn.

As they left Emily's tiny flat, she explained, "She's an American, entertaining with a USO troupe here. She came over to be closer to her husband, who's in the army. She just got word recently that he's missing in action. Presumed dead."

His immediate thought was a selfish one. He was glad he hadn't known this soldier, hadn't had the responsibility of notifying his next of kin. That was the worst of his duties: he performed it with all the grace of someone who'd had good manners drummed into him from childhood, and then promptly got drunk in an effort to erase the memory of shocked, grieving faces.

"She's a nice girl," Emily went on as they walked outside. "She puts on a brave front, but sometimes at night I hear her crying."

"How did you get to be flatmates?"

"Her flat was bombed, so she needed a place. And Margie, my previous flatmate, had just left, so I was looking for someone to share expenses. We started talking in the grocer's one day, and as soon as I discovered she needed a place, I invited her to move in."

"Without really knowing her?"

"We have a mutual friend, Rose Donovan. I don't think you've met Rose. She does war relief work. At any rate, I knew if Rose liked her, she must be all right. And she is. She's a bit common. I think she comes from a rather poor family. But she's a decided improvement over Margie, who was trying to set some sort of world's record for number of servicemen seduced at one/ten/A Grantland Place."

He smiled. "That must have played hell with your own plans to entertain dates."

She gave him a slow, thoughtful look. Finally she responded, "Oh, I don't entertain much, anyway."

"What's the matter? Don't the chaps you meet recognize a great girl when they see one?"

"Am I a great girl, Richard?"

"You are indeed. The man who gets you for a wife will be lucky."

"What makes you think so?"

He was surprised at her sudden lack of self-confidence. It wasn't like her to fish for compliments. He decided she must have a crush on someone who wasn't responding.

Putting his arm around her shoulder, he said, "I know you better than anyone does. You've been my best friend since we were both in nappies. So I know what a wonderful girl you are, Emily. Don't worry. Before you know it, someone will be smart enough to realize that."

She whispered, "I hope so."

As they skillfully maneuvered their way through the crush on the sidewalks, they made a striking pair—seemingly a perfect match. Both were blond-haired, blue-eyed and fair-skinned. Something about the way they carried themselves suggested their aristocratic lineage.

After standing in a long line, they finally boarded a bus that took them to the theater district in Piccadilly. The marquee at the Montfort Theatre read "USO Entertainment Nightly."

At the ticket booth Emily asked for the tickets that Jesse had left for her, then she and Richard went inside. The place was packed with servicemen from nearly all the Allied armies. Many had girls on their arms, mostly English, a smattering of Americans. They were laughing, talking, snuggling up to each other.

Overnight romance, Richard called it. He wasn't critical. He understood the motivation all too well. Fear and loneliness were powerful aphrodisiacs. It was easy to believe you were in love when you wanted desperately to believe it.

Then the lights dimmed and the curtain rose. The MC, a dapper Cockney, walked to center stage and the audience immediately quieted. After a little

humorous patter, which the audience responded to
enthusiastically, he announced the first performer:
Mrs. Jesse Cantrell, songstress from the American
South.

As he walked offstage a spotlight came on, high-
lighting the simplest of props: a microphone, a chair
and a cardboard backdrop of a curtained window
overlooking a park. A young woman walked on-
stage, and the audience clapped wildly and whistled.

She was a stunner all right, Richard thought.
Petite but curvaceous, with the most magnificent red
hair like a fiery halo around her pale, oval face. She
wore a simple black dress with a white lace jabot
cascading down the front. Modified mourning? he
wondered.

But if she was in mourning, she didn't let it show.
As the orchestra struck up a lively tune, her eyes
sparkled and she flashed an impudent smile at the
audience. Then she sang a saucy little number.

> "I've got a cozy flat.
> There's a place for your hat.
> I'll wear a pink chiffon negligee gown.
> And I do know my stuff,
> But if that's not enough,
> I've got the deepest shelter in town."

The audience roared lustily with each chorus.
Jesse swayed in time to the music and occasionally
sat pertly on the chair, crossing shapely legs. When
she finished and bounced offstage, everyone ap-
plauded appreciatively.

"Come on," Emily shouted to Richard over the
noise from the audience. "Let's go."

"Are we going backstage?"

"No, it isn't allowed. But I told her we'd meet her at the pub across the street for dinner."

The pub was called the Half-Moon, for Half-Moon Square just outside. It was packed, but Richard managed to find a small table and three chairs in a corner. The barmaid had just brought a bottle of champagne in a bucket of ice when Jesse came in.

She stood just inside the doorway for a moment, looking for Emily. There was nothing saucy about her now, Richard thought. She looked small and helpless and rather appealing. He felt something odd happening deep inside him, as if his entire body had gone perfectly still for an instant. Suddenly he realized that he'd been holding his breath.

Emily caught Jesse's eye and motioned to her to join them. In a few seconds she'd made her way through the crowd and sat down.

Emily gave her a bright smile. "We saw your performance, Jesse. You were marvelous. By the way, this is the friend I told you about. Lord Richard Bredon, Jesse Cantrell."

"How do you do, Mrs. Cantrell?" he murmured politely, extending his hand.

She took it and at the same time gave him a disconcertingly direct look. For one endless moment their eyes locked. Awareness flooded through him. Awareness of her perfume, sweet and subtle . . . awareness of the incredible softness of her palm against the roughness of his . . . awareness of a sudden startled look in those tawny eyes.

When she finally spoke, her tone was gently mocking. "Pleased to meet you, Lord Bredon. You know, you're my second aristocrat. To meet personally, that is. Emily was the first."

"Oh, bosh," Emily said with a grin. "She's having you on, Richard. It's that peculiar American sense of humor."

His gaze remained on Jesse. "Well, we're even, Mrs. Cantrell. You're the first singer I've met."

"Oh?"

"You're very good."

"Thank you."

Still their eyes met. Finally she lowered her gaze.

Richard felt he'd won a battle of wills, somehow, in forcing her to be the first to break eye contact. She might be small and vulnerable-looking, but, he decided, she wasn't soft. There was a toughness there, probably from the war. It was a toughness he respected.

"Were you a professional singer in the States?"

"No. My family was very musical, though self-taught. I auditioned for this USO troupe and performed in public for the first time when I was accepted into it."

"Were you nervous?"

The corners of her full mouth curved slightly in a self-mocking smile. "Of course. But I didn't let it show."

No, he thought, you wouldn't.

Emily's gaze flicked from Richard to Jesse and back again. Her smile seemed rather forced, Richard thought idly, as she said, "Well, drink up, everyone. Mustn't let this bubbly go to waste."

"Right you are, Emily." He filled all three glasses to the brim. Then, as they raised their glasses, he said, "A toast is in order. Who'll give it?"

Emily answered, "You, Richard. You do it so beautifully."

"That's only at family occasions, when we're drinking to my parents' health. I'd like Mrs. Cantrell to give this toast, if she will."

"All right." She held her glass up. "To the end of this terrible war. It can't come too soon."

They clinked glasses.

As Jesse slowly sipped the champagne, Richard watched her. "I understand why you've had enough of this war, Mrs. Cantrell. Emily told me about your husband."

Tears glistened at the corners of her eyes, but he knew she would fight them back. He'd seen that kind of quiet gallantry often enough to recognize it immediately. Though he'd only just met her and knew very little about her, he was certain of one thing. This woman had courage.

She looked away, not speaking. Her hands lay crossed on the edge of the table. He reached out and covered them with his own hands for just a moment. As he did so, she started to pull back instinctively, then she stopped and left her hands under his.

His voice was a whisper. "It's all such a bloody waste."

She looked up at him through thick golden lashes. *"Yes."*

Their eyes met in perfect understanding.

For the remainder of the evening, they talked about everything except the war. Emily was her usual bright, breezy self. Richard, however, was quiet. Occasionally he found himself lapsing into silence and staring at Jesse. She seemed to be forcing herself to be congenial. He sensed she didn't want to be in the noisy, crowded pub, drinking champagne and pretending to have a good time.

Because of air raids, the pubs closed early, at ten

o'clock. At that time, Richard escorted Emily and Jesse back to their flat.

"Are you heading back to the base tonight?" Emily asked.

"Yes, unfortunately."

"Well, do stop by when you get your next leave. It's always wonderful seeing you."

"I will." Turning to Jesse, he said, "It was a pleasure, Mrs. Cantrell."

She nodded. He could see the exhaustion in her face, etched in fine lines at the corners of her eyes and mouth, and he understood all too well: it took a tremendous effort to hide your emotions.

But when she spoke there was the suggestion of a fragile, dawning expectancy in her voice. "Take care, Lord Bredon."

"I will."

As he left he felt oddly light. Jesse Cantrell brought out in him feelings of tenderness and vulnerability that he'd suppressed because of the war. It was exhilarating to feel again, to not just perform by rote the outward gestures of living.

"Take care," she'd said. Now he felt as if there might be something to be careful for. . . .

Casey let herself into her room at the Viscount Hotel. "Moderately priced," the travel agent back home had said. "Moderately priced" meant a room so small it was barely large enough for a single bed, inadequate dresser and one worn chair next to a tiny round table with a brass lamp that badly needed polishing. And no private bathroom.

But it *was* located within walking distance of Piccadilly Street, where Casey had learned Richard Bredon had an office.

At the moment she wasn't concerned about the dreary inadequacies of the room. Kicking off her shoes, she leaned back against the scratched wooden headboard and thought about her disappointing interview with Bredon.

She'd expected him to read the letter immediately and, perhaps, share its contents with her. At the very least she'd expected some kind of explanation.

Instead he'd lied about ever knowing her mother, had shown real dislike of Casey herself for no apparent reason and had unceremoniously kicked her out, after making it clear he never wanted to see her again.

Again she wondered *why*. She certainly wasn't a threat to him, at least as far as she knew. Yet that was precisely how he'd reacted to her. The moment she'd mentioned her mother's name, he'd reacted with bitter animosity. How could anyone feel that way about her mother? Jesse Cantrell had been a quiet, sweet, gentle woman who'd never made an enemy in her placid, uneventful life.

Casey took a stack of papers from the open suitcase lying on the floor next to the bed. On top was a framed photograph of her and her parents taken the Christmas before last. It was just a small photo taken by an Instamatic camera. It was even a little blurred, because the friend who'd taken it had drunk a bit too much mulled wine beforehand and was none too steady. But it was the only photo Casey had of her parents and herself together since she'd graduated from high school.

Casey and her mother sat next to each other with arms interlocked, flanking her father, a thin, gray-haired man who looked older than his sixty-five years. He was smiling sheepishly into the camera, and from the blurred picture it was almost impossible to tell that he was in a wheelchair.

Casey swallowed past a lump in her throat as she remembered his quiet courage. He'd never complained, never betrayed the slightest hint of bitterness at his disability. Despite overwhelming obstacles, he'd managed to earn a modest living from the farm he'd inherited from his parents. He'd been embarrassingly proud of his wife and daughter and had insisted until the day he'd died that he was a very lucky man.

Casey turned to her mother. Instead of looking into the camera, Jesse's eyes were on her husband. She looked, as usual, devoted and concerned. Casey had always thought her mother looked exactly like what she was—a middle-aged farmer's wife. She didn't use makeup and wore simple, slightly outdated clothes because there wasn't enough money to keep up with the latest fashions.

Now, Casey stared intently at the woman in the photo, trying to see beyond the almost stereotypical surface. Obviously there must be more to her mother than she'd assumed, since somewhere in her mother's history was a relationship with a wealthy, aristocratic Englishman.

Casey shook her head, thoroughly confused. *Her* mother? It didn't seem possible. Yet as she looked at the photo she realized that her mother *was* very attractive. In her youth, Casey knew from old photos, she had been a real beauty.

But as far as Casey was aware, Jesse had never left the United States. She'd never even left Kentucky. She'd occasionally talked about wanting to visit a cousin in California. But travel was difficult for Casey's father, and they'd never made the trip.

Yet somewhere, sometime, Jesse Cantrell had met Richard Bredon. And whatever their relationship, it was important enough that she wanted to communicate with him after her death.

Once more Casey picked up the sealed letter and stared at it curiously. She'd been tempted from the first to open it. Now, after being rebuffed by Richard Bredon, she was even more tempted. After all, if he didn't want it . . .

Besides, she couldn't simply throw it away. Maybe whatever was in it concerned something she could deal with.

But even as her mind struggled to find logical reasons why it would be all right, even necessary, to open the letter, Casey knew it would be wrong to do so. Her mother had been soft-spoken and far from authoritative, but she'd believed very strongly in certain principles. Privacy was one. She'd never once read a letter addressed to Casey or pried into personal matters. Even during Casey's turbulent teenage years, when she had temporarily taken to smoking and drinking in an effort to look more "mature," her mother hadn't searched her room for evidence of wrongdoing.

Her mother had respected her right to privacy, and Casey knew that she could do no less now in return.

With a sigh of frustration, she put the letter back in her suitcase along with the photo.

But she wasn't about to give up. Picking up the telephone, she dialed the reception desk and asked where she might go to find information about the English aristocracy.

"*Debrett's Peerage,* miss," the East Indian clerk answered in heavily accented English. "There's sure to be one in the lending library near here."

After getting directions, Casey put on her damp raincoat and went out once more.

Debrett's was surprisingly helpful. The long paragraph on Lord Richard Bredon read succinctly:

BREDON, Richard Carlisle, D.S.O; born 1921, 2nd son of James Montgomery Bredon, 15th Baron of Bellingham, and Claire Cavendish, daughter of Sir Henry Cavendish of Rose Hill Manor, Hants. Succeeded to the title upon the death of his elder brother, Roger, killed in combat in 1942. Married 1944, Lady Emily Louise Harrison, daughter of the Marquis of Elmbury; one son (Michael Cavendish Bredon) born 1945.

Educated: Eton College and Balliol College, served with H.M. Forces 1941/46 (Lieutenant, RAF).

Residences: Bredon Hall, Middlesex; No. 12 Fairfield Court, Belgravia.

Arms: Sable, a boar courant, argent; crest, two lions in combat, proper.

Two lions in combat.

Casey unhooked the clasp of her necklace and held up the pendant. Two lions rose up against each other, their tails thrashing in the air, claws extended menacingly, teeth bared.

No wonder Lord Bredon had looked startled when she'd pulled out the pendant and fiddled with it nervously. It was his family crest. How on earth had Jesse Cantrell come to possess it?

Casey tried to remember what her mother had

said about it when she'd given it to Casey ten years ago. Casey had been helping her mother clear out the attic when she'd run across a small velvet bag tied at the top with a silk ribbon. Opening it, Casey had found the pendant and chain.

"What's this—an old family heirloom?" she had joked.

Her mother had picked up the pendant and stared at it in silence for a long moment. Finally she'd whispered, "Yes, it's an heirloom."

"It looks kind of valuable."

"It is."

"Why don't you wear it?"

"No." Her mother had given it back to her and said, "You wear it, honey."

"Are you sure?"

"Yes. I'm sure."

Now Casey ran a finger lightly over the embossed gold medallion.

Oh, Mom. Why didn't you tell me the whole truth about this? What secret were you guarding?

That evening after dinner, Casey considered what she should do next. Approaching Lord Bredon again directly was out of the question. She'd written down the two addresses listed for him in *Debrett's,* but she had no idea what to do with them. Showing up at either of his homes wouldn't do any good. Unless . . .

She thought furiously for a moment. Bredon Hall was obviously his family seat. There might be someone there, perhaps an old servant, who knew of Bredon's relationship with her mother. She didn't have much money, but at this point she was willing to use what little she did have to bribe someone for information.

Looking at a map of London and its environs, she found that Middlesex was just northwest of London, not far from Heathrow Airport. She could rent a car and be there in two hours.

She decided to leave first thing in the morning.

A tiny voice inside her said naggingly, You're playing at being a detective. And you don't know the first thing about it. But the alternative to this plan—failing to deliver the letter as her mother had wished—was unacceptable.

Feeling more than a little like a fool headed on a wild goose chase, she went to bed.

The next morning she set off in an English Ford. Driving on the left was awkward and occasionally problematic, and the fact that it was still raining made it even worse. She breathed a heartfelt sigh of relief when the heavy traffic of London was behind her. After half an hour of clenching the steering wheel tightly, her hands were beginning to ache.

Driving west, she passed through Hounslow. According to the guide book she'd consulted, it had once been called Hounslow Heath and was notorious for the highwaymen haunting the main west road out of London. Now it looked like nothing more than a dull suburb.

To the south was the vast expanse of Heathrow Airport. The small villages surrounding it were surprisingly rural in atmosphere and quite charming. The countryside was lush—green, dotted with trees bordering an occasional meandering stream.

Looking around her, Casey experienced a wave of nostalgia. The bluegrass country of Kentucky, where her small farm was located, was every bit as lush as this. She wished she were there now. Unfortunately, however, she had made arrangements to visit London for two whole weeks—had gone to the trouble and expense of securing her tickets and hotel room; had packed enough for a two-week stay as a tourist; and had left the farm in the care of her foreman, a trustworthy old geezer who'd been her father's right-hand man for over twenty years.

She'd made all these arrangements so she could take a long overdue vacation, but already she was beginning to feel she didn't really want to be here. In fact, she was beginning to suspect she'd arranged this "vacation" simply to justify traveling all the way to London to deliver her mother's letter—to a man who obviously had no desire to receive it . . . or her.

Casey squared her shoulders determinedly. If Lord Bredon had no intention of unraveling the mystery behind her mother's last request, she'd just have to find it out for herself some other way . . . even if it took her the whole two weeks.

She stopped in the ancient market town of Uxbridge, and asked at a tourist office for directions to Bredon Hall.

"I'm sorry, but Bredon Hall isn't open to the public, miss," the young information officer, a plump brunette, replied. She delivered the information with what Casey was sure must be her patented friendly-smile-for-the-tourists.

"I'm aware of that. I'm going there on personal business."

Casey was afraid the girl would ask, "Then why on earth don't you know the way?"

Fortunately she didn't seem to have a very questioning nature. She simply said, "Oh, in that case I'll indicate the route on this map here. You can't miss it. It's just down the road a bit. It's one of the finest old homes in Middlesex."

A few minutes later, Casey pulled her car onto the grass verge at the edge of a narrow, private road and stared at a small brass plaque that read Bredon Hall. Through a black wrought-iron gate, she could see the beginning of a winding drive bordered by thick trees. But that was all she could see of the place. A tall brick wall and a small forest of trees totally obscured the estate.

"Damn!" she muttered irritably.

Nothing was going right. But she hadn't come all this way just to turn around and go back without even seeing the place. Slowly she drove farther on, skirting the wall, looking for a gap in it.

Finally she found one. Not exactly a gap, but a place where a tree limb hung over the wall. It looked as if it might be low enough for Casey to reach it and climb up onto the wall.

Pulling her car off the road, she got out. The rain was just a wet mist now, and she left her raincoat in the car. She was glad that she'd worn jeans and a sweater. It would make climbing easier.

As a child, she'd climbed a lot of trees. Her mother had disparagingly referred to her as a hopeless tomboy. She'd eventually grown out of it, but it came in handy now. Grabbing the sturdy limb, she hoisted herself up onto the wall.

Then, holding on to the limb for balance, for the top of the wall was narrow, she looked out onto Bredon Hall. The trees near the wall thinned out to a huge grassy park sweeping up to elaborate, formal gardens. Beyond the gardens, a stone terrace surrounded the house itself.

The house was magnificent. Built of red brick, it was three stories tall, with a two-story wing on either side. Tall, mullioned windows glinted in the soft autumn sunlight that was beginning to break through the overcast sky. Smoke drifted out of two of several chimneys.

Casey knew little of architecture, but she thought this was probably Queen Anne. The lines were simple and graceful. Everything about it—the house itself, the gardens, the aura of peace and quiet—was incredibly lovely.

"What the bloody hell do you think you're doing?!"

Startled, Casey lost her grip, grabbed desperately for another limb, missed and fell.

Chapter Two

The man who'd shouted at her broke Casey's fall. She came down with too much force to be neatly caught in his arms. Instead he grabbed her, then twisted sharply so that when they fell onto the ground together, he was underneath.

Still, the impact was hard, and she felt her breath knocked out of her. This had happened to her before, when she'd taken a bad spill while riding. But that didn't make it any the less scary now.

Gasping desperately, she fought for breath.

The man turned her over so that she lay with her back on the ground. "Don't panic, you'll be all right. Just breathe deeply."

The voice, very deep, very male and irritatingly condescending, angered her. She wanted to respond, "I *never* panic!" But she couldn't get the words out.

Though it galled her to follow his orders, she knew he was right. So she lay back and took in deep breaths of cool, damp air tinted with the woodland scent of moss and fallen leaves.

After a moment the fear of suffocating passed, and the sudden, awful terror of falling was replaced by an overwhelming relief. She was all right.

Then she became aware that her arms and legs were tangled with the man's. He held himself above her, putting most of his weight on one elbow, his other arm spanning her waist. His position, half on her, half on the ground, was intimate in the extreme. Through her worn jeans, Casey felt his long, muscled leg thrust between hers. Through her sweater, she felt the hardness of his chest almost, but not quite, crushing her breasts as they rose and fell heavily while she tried to suck in air.

Her vulnerable position brought on a renewed feeling of panic. "Let me go," she demanded in a breathless whisper that was all her voice could manage at the moment.

"An American tourist. I might have known. No one else would be so pushy." The upper-class accent dripped sarcasm.

She started to respond angrily to the insult; then she looked up into his eyes and her angry response was cut off. They were blue, but that simple word didn't begin to describe them. Turquoise was closer, but even that didn't capture their clear intensity. Silver and gold glinted in the pale blue and gave his eyes a constantly changing, mysterious quality. Casey felt she could look into those eyes forever and still not quite understand the man himself.

At the moment, however, the expression in them was more than clear—unabashed fury. As she continued to stare, the fury slowly softened, almost imperceptibly, to a dawning curiosity.

Realizing that her gaze had been locked with his for far too long, she forced herself to pull back. In doing so, she took in the rest of his face. It was arresting rather than handsome—a straight, aristocratic nose, high cheekbones and a mouth that was firm but full. His lips were clenched tightly in a frown. But in the way they curved up at the corners there was a suggestion of humor that was very appealing.

A lock of hair the deep gold of ripe wheat fell rakishly across a wide forehead. His skin was the darker gold of honey. Everything about him—his eyes, skin and hair—seemed blessed by sunlight.

Casey thought erratically, He should be on a Caribbean island or a Southern California beach, not in England on a misty autumn day.

This was a man she would notice under any circumstances. Under different circumstances, she would find him very intriguing. Under her present, vulnerable circumstances, she found him more than a little intimidating.

He shifted his leg slightly and Casey felt it brush along the inside of her thigh. At that instant, something deep within her that had lain tightly coiled and untouched for a very long time quivered as if slowly being brought back to life. The purely physical reaction caught her off guard and sharpened her fear.

"I said let me go!" Her voice was shaky, and she had to bite her lower lip to keep it from trembling.

"No." The tone was perfectly calm and absolutely rigid.

"What?"

"It's a bit late to go all irate and innocent, young woman. I have no intention of letting you scramble back over that wall the way you came. You damned tourists get worse every year. Hampton Court and the Tower of London aren't enough for you. You think you can invade anywhere. An Englishman's home may be his castle, but not every castle is open to tourists."

"I'm not a tourist!"

"Well, you're certainly not someone who has any right to be here. You're trespassing and I intend to hand you over to the local magistrate."

"Magistrate! But I didn't intend to trespass. If you hadn't yelled at me . . ."

"You wouldn't have fallen? Perhaps not. But you would have continued invading my privacy in your determination to get a look at my home. You're lucky I broke your fall instead of letting you land flat on your face."

Casey decided it was long past time to inject a note of reason into this ludicrous conversation. "If you'll just let me explain . . ."

"Explain what? Why you were spying at my home?"

Her temper blew, and with it went all concern for her helpless position. "Why, you rude, overbearing, arrogant, condescending . . ." She searched for the worst possible epithet and finally settled on, "Englishman! You can take your precious house and stuff it!"

He'd been prepared for embarrassment, confusion, even tearful pleading. But not anger. The woman was surprising. And since it had been a long time since he'd met a woman with the ability to surprise him, he took another, harder look at her.

He hadn't particularly noticed her appearance before. Now he realized hers was a subtle attractiveness. At first glance she merely looked pretty, in an unmade-up, fresh-scrubbed sort of way. But the longer he looked at her, the more he appreciated her natural, unaffected beauty.

Her tawny eyes were almond-shaped and fringed with golden-brown lashes that were soft and thick. Her skin was pale, yet had a subtle glow, like the finest porcelain. Her nose, with its smattering of golden freckles, was cute. But that mouth—it was a great deal more than merely cute. It was incredibly sensuous and inviting.

And her hair—it was a more dazzling bronze than the fallen leaves that were entwined in it. It was so long and thick it nearly overwhelmed that piquant face. The loose tendrils lay in glorious disarray. Just as it would look, he thought, on a pillow after she'd made uninhibited love to someone.

Her body was soft and pliant. Beneath the thin, forest-green sweater was molded the generous outline of full breasts. As he looked down at her, as helpless as a butterfly beneath him, fifteen generations of feudal privilege stirred in his blood.

There was more than a little of the voluptuous milkmaid about her—and he was, after all, an aristocrat. He felt an earthy attraction to her as ancient as his family's title. His expression softened and the arm that spanned her narrow waist pulled her even closer against him.

His voice lowered to a huskier tone. "On second thought, perhaps turning you over to the magistrate would be a shameless waste. He's over seventy, and probably incapable of appreciating what he'd be getting."

"Why, you . . . you . . ."

One blond eyebrow rose quizzically. "Englishman? I believe that was the worst thing you could think of to call me a moment ago. As an insult, it at least has the virtue of being accurate."

Casey's left hand was free. She raised it to push him off. Instead he grabbed it by the wrist and held it effortlessly. A sly grin softened the passion that had been all too evident in his expression. "What's this, playing hard to get? You can't pretend you haven't fallen for me."

Despite herself, Casey felt an irresistible urge to laugh. Though she hadn't felt much like laughing lately, she was normally as quick to laugh as she was to get angry. Her strong temperament worked freely both ways.

Now she tried to force down the laughter that bubbled up within her. But it was no good. The dry humor and wry grin were irresistible. The corners of her wide mouth turned up in a smile, then she laughed softly.

He smiled down at her. "I'm Michael Bredon. You're . . ."

"Still lying on the rather wet ground."

"Ah, yes. I'd forgotten your unfortunate position."

"Had you?" she responded dryly as he helped her up.

They both brushed off leaves and dirt. Then Casey looked at the man standing only inches from her. He was medium tall—perhaps five feet ten or so. But she was so short in her flat-heeled boots that he towered over her. He wore an old, almost shabby, yet extremely well cut charcoal-colored tweed blazer over a close-fitting gray turtleneck and matching slacks. He was lean, with the kind of taut, elegant body that looked good in everything from a tuxedo to jeans.

Casey had never been any good at all at hiding her feelings. Whether she was sad or happy, friendly or disapproving, it was there on her countenance for all the world to see. Now, as she looked into his eyes once more, she realized with a flush of intense embarrassment that he was aware she was eyeing him favorably.

As he met her unabashed scrutiny, his smile broadened to a killer grin that made her catch her breath. She remembered something she'd heard once about being seduced by the stranger with the flashing smile. This stranger definitely was seductive.

Then she remembered he wasn't a stranger. He was Richard Bredon's son. Suddenly her humor vanished.

"I didn't intend to trespass, Mr. Bredon. If you'll show me the way out . . ."

"I'm not about to let you off that easily."

Her temper flared. "Are you taking me to the magistrate after all?"

"No. I told you, he wouldn't appreciate his good fortune."

"A gentleman would—"

"Certainly do as you suggest," he interrupted blithely. "But who said I'm a gentleman?"

"You live like one. You talk like one. You even dress like one. Only a gentleman could afford to wear something so shabby."

He feigned a hurt expression. "Hold on, there. On behalf of my tailor, I protest. This is my favorite coat."

"And your oldest, probably."

"Probably."

Noticing a gate in the distance, Casey turned and began walking quickly toward it. She threw back over her shoulder, "I'll let myself out."

He caught up with her quickly. "I must warn you, the gate's locked. Of course, with your agility as a climber, that should pose no problem."

Casey felt embarrassment wash over her once more. She was trying desperately to get out of this awkward situation with some semblance of dignity. It didn't look as if she would succeed.

She glanced at him, then looked away and kept walking. "If you'll just tell me how the hell I can get out of here, I won't trouble you any further."

"But you went to such lengths to get in. Why leave so soon? Since you've shown such an interest in my home, why not let me show it to you?"

"I told you, I didn't intend to come onto the grounds."

Curiosity lit those pale blue eyes. "Why were you so anxious to look over the place, anyway, Miss . . ."

She didn't want to give him her name. But she knew there was no point in trying to lie—those piercing eyes would see through it in an instant.

"I don't think there's any need for you to know my name, since we'll never be meeting again."

"How can you be so sure of that?"

"I doubt we travel in the same circles," she replied sarcastically.

"I don't know about that. I've been known to shop at Harrods and dine in Soho—places no self-respecting tourist would miss."

When Casey didn't respond, he went on, "Your

secretiveness is very mysterious. Makes me wonder if you might not be a cat burglar after the famous Bredon silver."

Without looking at him, Casey asked with what she hoped was withering sarcasm, "Do I look like a cat burglar?"

He didn't answer at once. Finally he said, "You don't look like anyone I can neatly categorize. That's what makes you so intriguing." His tone was so provocative Casey couldn't resist flashing a quick glance at him.

At the gate, Casey stopped and faced him. Gesturing, she said, "Will you open it, please?"

He considered her request for a long moment.

Losing patience, she said, "Well?"

"Just a moment. I'm trying to decide if it would be worth it to watch you climb over it."

"If that's an attempt at humor, it isn't funny."

"No?"

"No."

He looked at her thoughtfully. "You don't like being teased, do you?"

"Does anyone?" she shot back.

His blue eyes softened with compassion. "No, I suppose not." Pulling a small brass key from his pocket, he unlocked the gate. "I was planning on going out this way on my walk. You're lucky. If I'd chosen a different route, you'd have had to walk half a mile to the main gate."

Casey went through the gate and turned in the direction of her car. She wasn't at all surprised that Michael Bredon walked beside her.

She reached her car in a minute and got inside. But before she could close the door, he leaned on it. "Why won't you tell me your name?"

"I explained why. We won't be seeing each other again."

Pulling the door gently but firmly, she closed it, then started the engine. But as she drove off, she heard him say, "Oh, yes, we will."

Michael ran an expert hand down the filly's right foreleg. Lowering her head, she blew playfully on his neck. "Cheeky," he said with a grin as he straightened up and rubbed her velvety muzzle.

He turned to the small, wizened man standing next to him. "She seems to be completely healed."

The little man, who wore a jaunty red cap over his sparse gray hair, nodded. "O' course. I been treatin' her like a princess. I didn't get to be head groom by not knowin' how to cure a sprained tendon." Then his faded green eyes narrowed. "Though I don't know why I bothered, seein' as how you'll be turnin' her over to that there foreigner."

"That there foreigner," Michael mimicked, "paid a tidy sum for her. This *is* a breeding farm, remember."

"In yer grandfather's day, horseflesh like this wouldn't be sold."

"My grandfather could afford to run Bredon Stud as a diverting hobby. Death duties and the supertax have taken away that prerogative. We have to show a profit, Dan, as you well know."

"But did you have to sell her to a bleedin' foreigner?"

"The sport of kings is not just for the British elite. Thoroughbred racing is open to anyone with enough money now, including 'foreigners.' "

"Ruddy mushrooms," Dan commented tersely. The derogatory word "mushroom" referred to anyone who got involved in racing without knowing anything about it, lost dismally, then got out of it.

Thoroughbred racing had become a target for the newly rich and for corporations, who saw it, correctly, as a means of unloading part of their wealth and in the process receiving free publicity. With their mystique and social entrée, thoroughbreds were an excellent way to ignite public interest in a tycoon—and gave him a chance to mingle with the high society that might otherwise ignore him.

Each season an army of newcomers came in like lions and, within a couple of years, went out like lambs. Men brilliant in their own businesses too often tried to employ their strategies in a world alien to them, with laws unto itself.

It was Michael's world, one he'd grown up in, understood and loved.

He said thoughtfully, "Hamdan al Dubai is no *mushroom.* He's putting together the finest stud farm in England."

"Well, all the money he can earn from his oilfields won't buy anything like Bredon Stud," Dan insisted loyally. "Some things you can't buy."

Michael didn't argue. Despite his pragmatic approach to the business of breeding, training and racing thoroughbreds, in his heart he agreed with Dan. Some things—like the atmosphere of Bredon Stud—couldn't be bought.

He looked around him. In rows of whitewashed box stalls, some of the finest thoroughbreds in Europe stood placidly, hanging their heads over the open upper halves of the doors. In the paddock, a groom watched carefully while a rambunctious young gelding was walked by an exercise machine that pulled steadily on his lead rope.

In a distant pasture, yearlings tossed their heads, snorted and chased each other. In another year they would be racing as two-year-olds. And the age-old question—the question at the heart of racing— would be answered: Which of the carefully bred, high-strung, magnificent animals would have that elusive quality that made a champion?

Some people thought it was all breeding. But Michael knew better. He'd seen too many horses with flawless pedigrees come in dead last—and seen too many cheap upstarts who had nothing going for them but exceptional conformation surprise the experts by having that crucial will to win.

That quality was called "heart."

Now why, he wondered, was he suddenly reminded of that young woman with the gorgeous bronze hair?

Suddenly he realized Dan was talking. "What? I'm sorry, I wasn't listening."

"'Course not. You were probably thinkin' of some little bit o' fluff."

"She's little, but fluffy isn't the adjective I would choose. She's got too much temper for that."

Dan's face broke into a knowing smile. "Ah, finally met yer match, have you? 'Bout time. You're not gettin' any younger, y'know. Thirty-eight your last birthday, weren't you?"

"Thanks for reminding me. I'll see about getting a cane and spectacles."

"Laugh if you want, but I'm gettin' tired of waitin' for you to settle down and provide an heir for all this. I have nightmares about this place goin' to some foreigner."

"You're a fine one to talk. Sixty-three and still a

bachelor. And quite a way with the ladies, from what the lads tell me."

Dan grimaced. "Ah, go on with ye. If I'd found the right woman, I'd have settled down right enough. Since that blessed event never happened, there's no reason for me to waste away in loneliness, is there?"

Michael laughed. "There certainly isn't."

Glancing at the paddock, Dan said irritably, "That boy's walkin' that gelding too fast. I'd best see to it."

When he'd gone, Michael put the filly back in her stall, then headed toward the house. It was a mile-long walk, but he enjoyed it. It gave him time to think about the farm, the horses, the people who worked under him in his capacity as manager of Bredon Stud.

Yet for once, those things weren't on his mind. Instead he found himself remembering the way a pair of faded jeans had fit snugly over a red-haired young woman's rounded hips. The way her full breasts had thrust against a thin green sweater. And most of all, the strange mixture of surprise, fear and desire that had lit her tawny-brown eyes as he'd lain close to her.

There was a mystery there that had to do with more than just the name she'd refused to reveal. It was a mystery he intended to solve.

Casey gathered up her soap, shampoo and wash-cloth and left the bathroom. She would have given anything for a private bathroom, where she could luxuriate in a hot bath and mull over the events of this remarkable day. But the price of first-class

London hotel rooms being what it was, outrageous, made that impossible. Her work—boarding and training horses on her small farm—was enjoyable but not exactly lucrative. As it was, this trip would eat up most of her meager savings.

As she turned the corner to the hallway that led to her room, she was stunned to see a familiar figure lounging against her door. Instead of a shabby blazer, he wore a dark suit whose expert cut emphasized his broad shoulders and slim torso.

How on earth had he found her?

"Good evening, Miss Cantrell," he said politely.

She felt at a distinct disadvantage with her just shampooed hair falling in wet disarray and wearing a white terry-cloth robe and worn slippers. And she was uncomfortably aware that underneath the robe she wore nothing at all.

Her words were clipped. "What are you doing here?"

"I should think that was obvious. I'm waiting for you."

He had straightened up upon seeing her. But he still stood in front of the door.

Clutching her key nervously, Casey said, "Do you mind?"

"Of course not. Here, let me." He took the key from her hand before she realized what he intended and unlocked the door. Then he stood there, holding it open for her. "After you."

She didn't want to invite him into her small room, but she didn't want to stand out in the hallway arguing with him, either. Hurriedly entering the room, she dumped her bath things on the top of the dresser, then whirled around to face him.

"How did you find me?"

He closed the door behind him, then leaned against it. "I'd like to pretend it took brilliant deductive reasoning on my part. The truth is, you left your car rental form in plain sight on the dashboard. Your name and hotel were on it."

Damn, she thought, angry at herself for such stupidity. She was clearly no good at all at this cloak-and-dagger business.

"Mr. Bredon . . ." she began firmly.

"Yes, Miss Cantrell?" he replied with thinly veiled humor in his tone. "By the way, please call me Michael. I think two people who've lain in each other's arms should be on a first-name basis. May I call you Casey?"

She was determined to resist his easy charm. "You may not. And you've wasted a trip here. Please leave."

"But I just got here."

"I don't care. I didn't invite you and I don't want you here."

Ignoring her blunt dismissal, he said matter-of-factly, "You know, Miss Cantrell, it will be very difficult for us to develop any sort of relationship if we spend such brief periods of time in each other's company."

"I have no intention of developing any sort of relationship with you!"

"Why not?"

The question was totally unexpected . . . and strangely difficult to answer. She stood there, unable to respond.

She could mention her meeting with his father, but she didn't want to do that. She could say that she wasn't interested in him, but that wasn't the truth. The problem was, she was very interested in him—

and not just because he might be a source of information about his father's relationship with her mother.

"Well, if you can't think of a good reason, then I suggest we go out to dinner. You haven't eaten yet, have you?"

She hadn't. She wasn't particularly hungry earlier. Now, however, at the mere mention of food her stomach growled softly.

He smiled. "You need to be fed, obviously. I promise you I will do it well. In an hour, you can be full of Welsh rarebit and roast beef. How does that sound?"

It sounded wonderful. Her resolve to resist him was weakening fast. Besides, she thought, if she handled things right, she might be able to get some useful information out of him.

That was a good enough reason to go out with him. Suddenly she wondered why *he* wanted to go out with her. He certainly didn't strike her as the type of man who had any trouble finding female companionship. The way he'd held her that afternoon suggested he'd had a lot of practice. He was an English aristocrat, handsome, charming and wealthy. What did he see in a poor, unsophisticated American?

In her direct way, she decided to ask him. "What do you want?"

The question hung in the air between them for a split second, like a challenge. Then the humor that had lit his face slowly dissolved; silver sparks glinted in those turquoise eyes, and his mouth tightened as if he were holding himself in check.

In two strides he'd crossed the tiny room and stood looking down at her. It took all of her courage not to flinch, or step back, or lower her gaze from his. But her hands clenched tightly at her sides and her breath was unsteady.

"What I want," he said slowly, emphasizing each word, "is to untie that robe and pull you against me so that I feel your naked body pressed against mine. What I want is to bury my hands in your wet hair and smell its sweet, natural scent. What I want is a great deal more than you're ready to give at this moment. But I can be patient when I know something's inevitable."

Her golden eyes blazed with anger at his arrogance and presumption. "If you think it's *inevitable* that we will make love . . ." She tripped over the words, at once embarrassed, angry and more excited than she cared to admit.

"I know it is. And I'm not saying it out of overweening vanity. The moment our bodies touched this afternoon, something happened. I felt it within me. And I saw it in your eyes . . . in the way you trembled as I held you. We're going to make love all right. And soon, because whatever's going on between us has a very short fuse. In the meantime . . ."

He paused and took a deep breath to steady himself. When he went on, his voice was tinged with the humor he'd shown earlier. "I'll wait in the lobby while you change. Try not to take too long. I'm famished."

He turned and left, closing the door gently behind him.

For a long moment, Casey simply stood there, rooted to the spot. Her mind was a whirling vortex of conflicting emotions. Should she tell him to go to hell? Would he even pay any attention if she did?

And what about her determination to get to the bottom of her mother's relationship with Richard Bredon? Michael could conceivably be of invaluable help.

All right, she decided abruptly, I'll go out with him. I'll use him however I can to get the information I need.

Throwing off her robe, she slipped on panties and a bra, then rummaged through the clothes she'd brought for something suitable to wear.

But she had the uncomfortable sensation that in trying to use Michael Bredon, she was playing with fire. And was liable to get burned very badly.

Chapter Three

The restaurant was small, dimly lit and intimate. They sat next to a window overlooking the Thames, flowing swift and dark beneath the pale light of a quarter moon. There was more food than Casey could ever remember eating at one meal, and it was all delicious. A light, clear consommé to start with, then Welsh rarebit, filet of sole and thick slabs of rare roast beef with Yorkshire pudding.

By the time the waiter brought dessert—raspberry trifle—Casey felt she couldn't eat another bite. But a taste of the trifle persuaded her to make room for this one last course.

Over coffee, Michael looked at her thoughtfully. "You've hardly spoken throughout dinner."

Her eyes met his over the rim of the white porcelain cup. "Neither have you."

Even in the dim light of the restaurant, his turquoise eyes were intense with curiosity. "I've been too busy staring at you."

"So I noticed. Why?"

"I'm trying to understand you. There's something about you that I can't quite decipher."

"I'm pretty uncomplicated, actually."

"Somehow, I don't think so. I get the feeling there's something going on with you that . . ." He stopped, unsure how to continue.

Casey sensed that he was a man who rarely felt unsure and didn't quite know how to handle it. But she wasn't about to explain herself to him.

When she remained silent, he asked abruptly, "Why did you come with me tonight?"

"You didn't leave me much choice."

"I don't accept that explanation. You don't strike me as the type to be steamrolled into doing something you don't want to do."

"Maybe I was just plain hungry. A free meal is a free meal."

He shook his head slowly. "No. That's not it, either."

Before he could jump to the wrong conclusion, she said quickly, "I have no intention of going to bed with you."

"I know you don't." His mouth curved in a provocative smile. "At the moment. That's why I'm so curious as to why you came."

"It seems we're back to where we started, Mr. Bredon."

"It seems so, Miss Cantrell."

She grew irritable under that penetrating gaze. "You're staring at me again."

"As I said, I'm just trying to understand you. Not an easy task. Even after watching you closely for two hours."

"So, I've been studied, weighed and measured.

What conclusions have you come to after dissecting me so intently?"

"That's a very straightforward question."

"I'd appreciate a straightforward answer."

He paused, then gave her a thoughtful look. "There are two kinds of people in the world. Those who want the truth at any price, however painful, and those who prefer to keep their illusions. I've found that most people fall into the second category."

"I'm not most people."

"So I've concluded. Do you really want the blunt, unvarnished truth?"

"Yes." Her voice was soft but sure.

"Rather than flattery?" he pressed.

"Oh, yes. I can handle the truth, no matter how hard it is. It's *not* knowing—or being unsure what's real and what isn't—that I can't handle."

"Yes," he said slowly. "I understand that."

Setting down his coffee cup, he crossed his arms on the table and leaned toward her. For a few seconds he watched as the light from the single white taper in the center of the table bathed her in a soft, rosy glow. Her skin looked so eminently touchable that it was all he could do not to reach out and stroke it gently. But he knew she would shy away like a startled filly if he did, so he restrained the almost overpowering impulse.

But he told himself that very soon he would touch that satiny skin, feel it quiver and come to life beneath his fingertips.

When he spoke, his tone was direct and betrayed nothing of his feelings. "All right, this is what I've concluded. Your appearance is subtly deceiving. You're not conventionally beautiful. Your nose is too short and your face just a bit too round, though I suspect the right makeup would bring out your bone structure. And that dress is all wrong."

It was her best dress, an emerald-green velvet with a small ruffle of white lace at the high neckline and short, close-fitting sleeves.

"What's wrong with it?" Casey demanded.

"I know green's the conventional color for red-heads to wear, but you're not a conventional red-head. You'd look better in something that would contrast more with your milkmaid complexion. And since I suspect you have a remarkable figure beneath all that heavy material, I'd suggest something soft and clinging to show it off."

Casey flinched at the blunt assessment. Well, she thought dryly, I asked for it.

He went on, his voice suddenly soft and gentle. "And yet, despite your determination not to make the most of yourself, the longer I look at you, the more I like the way you look."

The combination of the frank compliment, the husky voice and the blatantly sensual look in his eyes made her heart start thudding. She couldn't have spoken if she'd had to.

Fortunately, he didn't seem to expect a response from her, for he went on, eyeing her thoughtfully. "You're bright. Bright enough to parry my questions, which you clearly don't want to answer. But you're not skilled at deception. Your feelings are all too apparent."

"What feelings?" As soon as the words were out of her mouth, she regretted them. But they couldn't be called back.

"The fact that you're as attracted to me as I am to you, for one."

She set down her empty cup and flashed him a withering look. "Modest, aren't you."

"Modesty has nothing to do with it. I have more than my fair share of shortcomings, but vanity isn't one of them."

"Oh?"

"Oh. Not every woman I meet finds me irresistible."

She was thoroughly irritated now. "And just what makes you think I do?"

"I admit you don't *want* to be attracted to me. But you are."

"Wait a minute . . ." she began angrily.

He shrugged with deceptive casualness. "You *did* ask what I thought."

"That was a mistake."

"Yes, it was. Why don't you want to be attracted to me?"

She wanted to say, I'm not attracted to you. You're incredibly conceited for thinking so.

But that was a lie, and there was no way she could utter it convincingly. He would see through it, anyway.

There was an unexpected gentleness in his expression as he went on, "Is it just me you object to, or all men?"

"That's a loaded question. However I answer, I'm saying that you're right in thinking I'm attracted to you. So I don't think I'll answer."

He was surprisingly agreeable. "All right, let's talk about something else."

Somehow, she didn't trust his easy capitulation. She suspected it was merely a delaying tactic.

He smiled. "*Casey* . . . an unusual name. How did you come by it?"

"It was my father's idea. It was his best friend's name. And he decided that when he had a child, whether it was a girl or a boy, he'd name it Casey."

"Your mother didn't object? I understand women have strong thoughts on the subject of babies' names."

"Perhaps. But my mother never objected to anything my father wanted."

"She sounds like the traditional sort of woman who believed in deferring to men's better judgment. You don't appear to take after her in that regard."

His face was perfectly straight, but there was a twinkle in those blue eyes. Casey knew he was teasing. Instead of being irritated by it, however, she found it amusing.

He went on, "Where are you from?"

Casey considered how much to tell him. Would it mean anything to him if she said Kentucky? She decided to find out.

"A little place called Morrow, Kentucky. Population five thousand and decreasing."

It seemed to mean nothing to him. There was no flicker of recognition in his eyes and his tone was polite but not terribly curious. "Why decreasing?"

"Most young people leave there eventually. There's not much opportunity for jobs. And as far as excitement goes . . . well, they roll up the sidewalks at night."

He flashed that killer grin and sent her pulse racing again. When he spoke, the deceptively innocent words seemed loaded with an underlying meaning. "And what do you do in Morrow, Kentucky, Miss Cantrell?"

For a moment her voice seemed to have caught in her throat. When she answered, her tone was less assured than she would have liked. "I have a small farm. I inherited it from my parents. Jesse and Frank Cantrell."

Neither her mother's name nor her father's seemed to have any meaning for him, either. Obviously, whatever had happened between Richard Bredon and her mother had been kept a secret from Michael.

"Any brothers or sisters?"

"No." That one word held a wide range of emotion. Like most only children, she'd grown up secure in the knowledge that she was very special to her parents, yet basically lonely. She'd watched with envy while her friends had boasted proudly of brothers, or shared clothes, secrets and problems with sisters. They had occasionally complained about their siblings and told her she was lucky not to have to deal with any. But she'd sensed that they wouldn't have traded places with her for the world.

She'd later realized that her loneliness had been a good part of the reason why she'd fallen so hard for Jamison Grey. But he was one person she didn't want to think about. She was glad when Michael changed the subject.

"Do you grow things?"

"No, I board and train horses."

"Ah, you're in the bluegrass country, then."

"Yes, but I don't deal with thoroughbreds. The horses I board are for pleasure riding only. And the training is basically limited to gentling young horses so adolescent riders won't break their necks on them."

"*Gentling* them?"

"Of course. You don't want to break a horse's spirit. You just want it to be well behaved."

"Good advice for people as well."

"Do you see yourself gentling me, Mr. Bredon?" she shot back.

"I see myself trying. Are you married or engaged?"

Taken aback by the point-blank question, she answered reluctantly, "No."

"Good."

"Mr. Bredon, let's talk about you for a change."

"I find you a more interesting subject. I already know all about myself."

"But I don't."

"Ah, so you're interested in me. That's a hopeful sign. What would you like to know?"

She wanted to know about his father, but she realized it would sound odd if she began by asking about him. So she decided to approach the subject obliquely.

"Has Bredon Hall always belonged to your family?"

"Always."

"Is there a title to go with the estate?"

"There is. Baron of Bellingham."

For the first time there was a half-embarrassed note to his voice. Casey sensed that he wasn't fond of the title for some reason.

Focusing on this one weakness in his otherwise formidable arrogance, she teased, "Should I be addressing you as *Lord* Bredon?"

"*No*. You should address my father that way. He seems to like it."

"And you don't?"

He shook his head slowly and with feeling. "No."

"Why not?"

"Because it's meaningless. It sets up an artificial sense of superiority."

Casey responded dryly, "You obviously don't need any artificial help in that regard."

To her surprise he laughed, a rich, deep, full-throated sound that had the couple at the next table glancing at him in surprise and curiosity.

"Touché, Miss Cantrell."

"By the way, it's *Ms.*"

"No, it's Casey. Which is what I intend to call you from now on. And you will call me Michael." He leaned forward and his voice dropped to a husky whisper. "Until we find more intimate things to call each other."

He reached out and covered her hand with his own. When she automatically pulled back, he took hold of it between both his hands, gently yet firmly. His strength surprised her. Judging by his lean frame, she hadn't expected it. The gentleness, too, was surprising. His entire demeanor was, for the most part, so arrogant that she wouldn't have expected him to be considerate enough to be gentle.

As if reading her thoughts, he said quietly, "There's nothing to be afraid of. I won't hurt you."

Angered by his ability to sense her feelings so perceptively, she spoke tartly. "I didn't think you would. May I have my hand back, please?"

"Why?"

"Because." That sounded like a stubborn five-year-old, so she added, "Please."

The "please" did it. Reluctantly he let go, and she put both her hands safely in her lap.

He gave her a carefully appraising look. "Who was he?"

"What do you mean?" But even as she asked, she knew exactly what he meant.

"The man who made you so skittish."

"Among my friends, I'm considered remarkably sensible and strong. Definitely not *skittish.*"

"Then your friends must all be women."

She gave an exasperated sigh. "Does it ever occur to you that you might be wrong about something?"

His eyes lit with amusement. "There is the odd occasion when I have a twinge of self-doubt. This isn't one of those occasions."

Trying to ignore the unsettling feeling that his look sent through her, she asked, "Do you spend your time walking over the grounds of your estate, or do you actually *do* something?"

The amusement in his eyes reached his mouth, curving it slightly. "I manage to keep busy. We have a thoroughbred breeding farm—Bredon Stud. I manage it."

Despite her intention of steering the conversation toward his father, she found this revelation interesting. "What do you do exactly—breed or race or . . ."

"Everything. We have brood mares. And two top stallions at stud. And when we get a likely-looking prospect, we race it. Are you interested in thoroughbreds?"

She smiled. "No one born and bred in Kentucky could help but be interested in them."

"The farm's only a mile from Bredon Hall. I'll show it to you tomorrow."

She started to refuse, then stopped. After all, she told herself, the better she got to know Michael, the more she would learn about his father. That the prospect of seeing him again wasn't exactly unwelcome to her was something she preferred not to dwell on.

"All right."

She caught a flicker of surprise in his eyes before he controlled it. It pleased her to think that he hadn't been prepared for her easy agreement.

"I'll pick you up at ten, then, if that's all right."

"Fine."

He shot her a questioning look, but she concentrated on her coffee, which the waiter had unobtrusively replenished.

"Tell me more about yourself," she urged.

"Where would you like me to begin?"

"The beginning. Your parents."

"My father's not a bad sort. A bit too much the lord of the manor sometimes, but he means well. I wish he could let his hair down and have some fun, instead of always taking everything so seriously."

"I suspect *you* don't have that problem."

He grinned in a self-deprecating way. "No. I try not to take things too seriously."

"Why not? Life's pretty serious, after all."

"Is it? It doesn't have to be, if you don't let it."

"If you're born with the proverbial silver spoon in your mouth, perhaps not."

"Meaning I'm a spoiled, pampered member of the privileged class."

"Yes." There, she thought, that'll show him bluntness works both ways.

But instead of acting insulted, he merely seemed amused. "You've fit me into a neat little stereotype. I wish I could do the same with you."

"I don't think it's a stereotype. Have you ever in your life had to worry about money? I don't mean enough money to buy a million-dollar colt you fancy, but enough money to buy food, pay the mortgage . . ." She stopped, then went on, "Of course, you probably don't have a mortgage on Bredon Hall."

"Actually, we do. Even the oldest families run into financial problems from time to time. For instance, my great-great-grandfather lost everything gambling in Bath, a notorious gambling den in his day. He was forced to marry an unattractive but wealthy widow to recoup."

"That doesn't sound so bad."

"You haven't seen the portrait of the lady that hangs in our library. She looks thoroughly sour-tempered, as if she weren't at all sure she made a good bargain. Then my grandfather nearly went broke entertaining King Edward when he stayed at Bredon Hall. Of course, the king required a great deal in the way of entertainment."

"It must be interesting knowing your family history in such detail. All I know about my family is that my great-grandparents all came from Scotland."

"Sometimes ignorance is bliss. It's not always an advantage knowing what you have to live up to—or what you have to live down."

He smiled and Casey found herself returning the smile.

I like him, she thought. I like him more than I expected to. And probably more than is wise.

"Do you have brothers or sisters?"

He shook his head. "Like you, I'm an only child. That's another thing we have in common, besides an interest in horses."

He leaned forward, crossing his forearms on the table. "Have you noticed the really striking similarities between us?"

"No. What about your mother? Is she serious, like your father?"

He leaned back in the chair. The body language alone told Casey she'd touched on a sensitive subject. "Very."

The word was so curt that it was clear he didn't want to talk about her. Which made Casey even more curious about her.

"Do you and your parents live at Bredon Hall?"

"Actually, I have a flat here in town. I go back and forth quite a lot. My father lives at the hall."

"And your mother?"

"Lives in a townhouse in Belgravia. They lead what is euphemistically referred to as separate lives."

"I see."

Michael motioned to the waiter for the check. When he'd paid the bill he said to Casey, "Let's walk off that meal."

She nodded agreement, and in a moment they were walking along the Thames embankment. The river was broad and dark beneath the nearly starless sky. Casey's head barely reached Michael's shoulder. The next time she was with him, she decided, she would wear the highest possible heels she could find. She didn't like feeling physically dwarfed by him.

"Oh, look!" Casey exclaimed excitedly. "Swans!"

Michael smiled. "Hard to believe, isn't it, on a dirty, muddy river like this. Do you care for swans?"

Casey nodded. "Oh, yes. They're . . . serene. The first thing I can remember longing for was a china swan in a gift shop window. It was pristine white, with a black beak and tiny black eyes, and its neck curved gracefully. I picked it up, and I can still remember my mother saying worriedly, 'Don't drop it.' It felt so smooth. I thought it was the most beautiful thing I'd ever seen, and I wanted it so badly I could almost feel it."

Michael turned to look at her as they walked slowly side by side. "Did you get it?"

Her voice was small and tinged with old disappointment. "No."

"Your parents wouldn't buy it for you?"

"They didn't have the money. Apparently it was very good china, not just a cheap plaster thing." Because the pain of desperately wanting something unattainable was still sharp, she tried to make light of it. "I had expensive taste for a six-year-old."

"What happened to it?"

"I looked in the shop window every time we went into town to make sure it was still there. One day it was gone."

His hand reached for hers and held it. Because his touch was comforting now, rather than intimate, she didn't pull away.

"Have you ever wanted something that badly, Michael? Something you couldn't have?"

He kept his gaze straight ahead, not looking at her. "Yes."

Something in his tone, more poignant than angry, warned her not to ask what it was.

They walked in silence for several minutes. Casey was glad she'd chosen a raincoat with a wool lining, for it was especially cold here by the river. She felt her cheeks growing pink with the cold and stuck her free hand in the pocket of her coat.

Somewhere in the distance a ship's horn blew, a long, mournful sound. Carlights flickered on a bridge.

"Is that the Tower Bridge?" she asked.

He chuckled softly. "You tourists think every bridge in London must be the Tower Bridge. *That,* my little Yank, is Westminster Bridge."

A young couple passed them, arm in arm, giggling softly. They were dressed in the most outrageous punk style—rainbow-colored hair cropped close to their heads, garishly colored clothes and worn leather jackets. They looked thoroughly silly, Casey thought, but there was something appealing in their exuberance.

They were happy, that's what it was, she decided. As if they didn't have a care in the world. Their only concerns were probably no more substantial than what color to spray their hair and which pair of unmatching socks to wear.

She felt a pang of envy. Unlike her, they weren't faced with a mystery whose meaning eluded them— And which they had no idea how to solve.

"What's wrong?"

Startled, Casey looked up to find Michael watching her.

"Nothing."

He didn't believe her. She hadn't really expected him to. "Something bothered you just then. What was it?"

Irritated with herself for being so transparent, she snapped, "It's nothing that's any of your business."

His eyes narrowed in frustration. "Every time I touch on anything personal, you close up."

She pulled her hand away from his and stuck it in her pocket. "You're too damn nosy."

"And you're too damn defensive. Are you going to let me know who you are?"

"You know who I am."

"I have a few scattered pieces of information about you. But there's something more, something you won't let me see."

"You have a real talent for being melodramatic. Have you ever thought about becoming an actor?"

"I'm not about to be diverted by insults. Stick to the subject."

"What subject?"

"There's an undercurrent here I don't understand. And I'm not referring to the sexual one. *That* I understand and intend to deal with."

"Oh, you do, do you?"

"I do."

Suddenly he stopped walking and put both hands on Casey's shoulders, forcing her to stop and face him. "Five minutes ago we were carrying on a pleasant conversation. You were even opening up a little, letting me see something of those feelings you guard so jealously. Now, we're shouting at each other. What happened?"

She could feel the strength in his hands even through her coat and dress. What would they feel like, she wondered, on her bare skin?

She forced down the thought, then stepped back so that his hands were no longer on her shoulders. "Obviously, we're not compatible. You'd better take back that invitation for tomorrow."

"The invitation stands." His tone was adamant, hard rather than friendly, as if he were challenging her to a duel rather than inviting her for a tour of his farm.

"It's late and I'm tired. I'd like to go back to my hotel now."

He nodded, then followed as she turned and

headed back the way they'd come. In his car, a Land Rover, Casey leaned back in the seat and closed her eyes. Jet lag was catching up with her. Suddenly she felt absolutely exhausted.

At least, she thought, she now understood his choice in cars. She'd expected him to drive something sleek and expensive, like a Jaguar. The Land Rover had been a surprise. Now that she knew what kind of work he did, it made sense. It was much more practical to drive around a farm in a sturdy vehicle like this.

Though it was amazingly comfortable, she thought drowsily as she leaned her head back against the leather headrest. The seats were soft and there was enough legroom to stretch out. It was almost like being in bed. A soft, cozy bed where she could sleep for hours. . . .

Michael cast a quick glance at Casey, then turned his attention once more to the road. Driving in London traffic required total concentration. Which was too bad, because he would have much preferred to take the opportunity to watch Casey while she slept.

Pausing at a stoplight, he gave her a longer look. In the dimness of the car, she looked almost ethereal —that pale skin contrasting in such a startling way with that vivid bronze hair. Asleep, her defensiveness was gone. She had the innocence and openness of a sleeping child.

A horn honked impatiently behind him. Returning his gaze to the road, he saw that the light had changed and he hadn't even noticed. As he pulled out into the intersection, he thought how Casey was full of contrasts—and not just physical ones. One minute she was outspoken and straightforward, saying exactly what she thought. The next she withdrew behind an impenetrable barrier.

No, not impenetrable, he decided. He would get past that barrier, one way or another.

As he drove through the heart of Piccadilly, past flashing theater marquees and advertising lights, it suddenly occurred to him he was more interested in this petite American than he'd been in any woman for a long time. He'd known a variety of women, and he'd been attracted to them in varying degrees. He'd even, once or twice, considered marriage, more because it was expected of him than because he was deeply in love.

Casey Cantrell was like none of those women. She didn't have their poise and sophistication. She didn't bother to be pleasant to him, to flatter him, to make herself available.

Yet he found himself liking her a good deal more than any of the women he'd known.

At another stoplight, he examined Casey objectively. Her face had character and, as he'd told her so frankly, a subtle attractiveness. But most men wouldn't turn to stare at her as she walked down a street. They wouldn't, at first glance, consider her beautiful. And he had always, carelessly, condescendingly, demanded beauty.

As they'd walked on the embankment, he'd noticed how she moved, with a kind of coltish grace. She had an unselfconscious freedom of movement that was appealing. Yet he'd known women—a ballerina, in particular—far lovelier in motion.

Her voice had a husky quality that sent his pulse racing. But it didn't compare to the singer he'd dated once for a whole year.

What was there about this particular woman that

drew him to her so strongly? Skin like cream, hair he longed to run his fingers through and a curious, tough quality to her mind that challenged him.

His first thought had been to get her into his bed as quickly as possible, to quench the fire she lit deep within him. He wasn't a man used to postponing satisfaction. But now he wanted more than that. He wanted to understand her. To know who had hurt her and why. To learn what she was trying so hard to keep hidden from him.

He suspected he could take her if he insisted. Despite her denials, she desired him every bit as much as he desired her. But her reluctant passion wasn't enough. He wanted her to come to him willingly. To make love to him as fully as he would make love to her.

He wanted everything from her that she could give a man. And he intended to get it.

They were at her hotel. As Michael pulled the car over to the curb, then shut off the engine, Casey came to with a start.

She looked lost for a moment, as if she couldn't remember where she was or how she got there. But as her eyes met his, recognition dawned and, with it, embarrassment.

"I didn't mean to fall asleep."

His smile was tender. "It's all right. I didn't take it personally. You're obviously tired. When did you arrive in London?"

"Yesterday morning."

"Ah, jet lag. It'll be a week before you fully adjust."

Straightening up in the seat, she said politely, "Well, thanks for the evening. I'll see you tomorrow."

But before she could make her exit, he was out of the car and opening the door for her.

"I'll walk you to your room."

"That isn't necessary."

"No, but in a third-class hotel like this, it's definitely advisable." This time there was nothing tender about his smile. It was pleasant but determined.

They walked through the nearly deserted lobby, up the stairs to the second floor, down the hallway to her room. All the while, Casey's heart thudded with an anticipation she didn't want to admit.

At her door she took out her key, careful to face away from Michael so he couldn't take it from her as he'd done earlier. Quickly she unlocked the door, then, turning to look at him, extended her hand.

"Thank you for dinner."

That intense blue gaze never left her face as he reached out to take her hand. Holding her eyes with his, he took her hand in both of his. But he didn't let it go. Instead he turned it over, raised it to his lips and kissed the inside of the wrist.

Casey felt a shiver run the entire length of her body, from her trembling lips to her curling toes. Her fingers clenched, but still he didn't release her hand. He rained feather-light kisses along the inside of her arm.

Not once did his gaze waver from hers.

His lips moved back to her hand. With excruciating slowness he took each of her fingertips in his mouth, one by one. His tongue flicked over them briefly, tantalizingly, in a gesture so erotic Casey felt her stomach tighten and her breath catch.

Then, and only then, did he release her hand.

"You're welcome."

He turned and walked away.

Chapter Four

Casey went through her clothes once more. She had absolutely no idea what to wear to see Bredon Stud. At her own farm she'd have worn jeans and a sweat shirt. Somehow she didn't think that would be appropriate attire for touring one of the top horse farms in England.

But she'd already rejected every conceivable outfit. The jeans and green sweater she'd worn yesterday were too reminiscent of her heady first meeting with Michael. The navy-blue corduroy pantsuit she'd brought to wear during the day was a little too formal for walking around in dirt and grass. And a dress was out of the question.

She glanced at her watch: it was a quarter to ten. She only had a few minutes. Somehow she didn't think Michael would be late.

Then an idea came to her. On her bed, she laid out her jeans, a white Oxford shirt and the blue corduroy jacket from her pantsuit.

Perfect.

In a flash she was out of her bathrobe and dressed. Just as she was pulling her brown leather boots over her jeans, there came a knock at the door. Jumping to her feet, she gave herself a final look in the small mirror over the dresser. She'd pulled her unruly hair back in a long braid in an effort to look composed, perhaps even reserved. But it hadn't worked: a few tendrils had escaped already and curled softly around her face. And her expression was anything but reserved. Excitement shone in the rosy flush in her cheeks and the dancing golden lights in her eyes.

The knock came again. Casey swore softly at herself for not being able to control her emotions, then hurried to open the door.

Michael was dressed in the shabby blazer he'd worn the day before. It fit him perfectly, and he looked thoroughly at ease in it, in a way he hadn't when he was dressed up at dinner. He also looked rangier, more male—and devastatingly sexy.

"Good morning, Casey."

His smile was bright and cheerful. He was clearly a man who rose early and enjoyed the morning.

"Good morning, Michael. Shall we go?"

He flashed a wry smile. "Not disposed to linger, I take it?"

She shook her head.

"All right, then. Let's go."

He held the door open for her. As she walked past him his eyes followed her lazily. When he spoke, his voice was a barely audible murmur. "It's incredible what you do for a pair of faded jeans."

It took all her self-control to ignore the remark. But she felt a jolt that went all the way down to her toes.

He took a shorter, more direct route to Bredon Hall than Casey had taken the day before, and they arrived in less than an hour. The farm was a mile beyond the house, in a lovely setting that touched Casey immediately.

Whitewashed stables and barns nestled against the base of a gently sloping hill. In the foreground were several paddocks, and in the distance, large white-fenced pastures. In one, mares grazed placidly. In another, yearlings gamboled.

It was similar to thoroughbred farms Casey had seen in Kentucky, yet there was a subtle difference in atmosphere. Bredon Stud, Casey sensed, had been here a very long time.

"How old is it?" she asked.

"As old as the house. Oh, most of the buildings aren't the original ones, of course. Still, for two and a half centuries horses have been born and bred here."

Casey shook her head in amazement. "Incredible."

"What do you think?" Michael asked as he turned into the long drive that led to the farm.

"It must give you a very special feeling to be part of something that has such . . ." Casey searched for the right word to convey her meaning and finally settled on, "History. Continuity, perhaps. I'm not sure what to call it."

"I know what you mean. And it does give me a special feeling. From the time I was a small boy, pestering the grooms, chasing the colts, I knew this was what I wanted to do with my life."

Casey tried to make her voice sound casual as she asked, "Does your father have much to do with it?"

"Not really. He's far too busy with the business

interests that support the hall, and the farm as well, to a certain extent. He cares about it, but it's not—"

"In his blood?" Casey interrupted with a knowing smile.

He returned her smile. "Exactly. I couldn't imagine going into an office each day as he does. This is where I want to be. I hated college because I felt it was a waste. It kept me away from here for three long years."

"I didn't go to college. My parents wanted me to, and to please them, I tried it for one semester. But I wanted to be working with horses. When I persuaded them I could earn a living at it, they gave in."

"Were they interested in horses?"

"My father was. Before he was injured in World War Two he was an assistant trainer at a big farm in Kentucky."

"My father was in the war, too. Of course, most of their generation were."

Casey sent him a startled look as a thought suddenly occurred to her. Had her father and Richard Bredon known each other in the war? Did her mother's letter have to do with their relationship, rather than a relationship between her and Bredon? But if so, why did she have the pendant? And why hadn't she written to Bredon when Casey's father had died, instead of leaving a letter that would only be found after her own death?

It was all thoroughly confusing.

They had reached the main building and Michael pulled the Land Rover to a halt. "This is where the offices and the grooms' quarters are."

They got out, and Casey stood looking around for a moment. It was a gorgeous fall day, crisp and cold.

The sky had cleared overnight, and there wasn't even a hint of rain. She stuck her hands in her jeans pockets and breathed in the wonderful country air, pungent with the varied scents associated with horses and farms.

Michael put his arm through hers. "Come on. I'll show you 'round the old place."

There was something at once possessive and gallant about the way he took her arm. Instead of shying from his touch, as she had done the night before, Casey relaxed and enjoyed it. It felt very comfortable somehow to be walking beside Michael, feeling the rough tweed of his jacket brush against her, smelling his special scent. His cologne was subtle and a bit musky. Very pleasant.

Glancing at him out of the corner of her eye, she thought what a distinctive profile he had. His face was lean but strong, his chin determined. As she'd noticed before, there was humor in the slightly upturned mouth. But while his eyes could glint mischievously, there was an underlying seriousness in them that was almost poignant.

Remembering their conversation the night before, she wondered what it was that Michael had wanted very badly and never gotten.

They had just reached the first row of box stalls when they met Dan.

"Miss Casey Cantrell, I'd like you to meet my head groom, Dan McGuire."

She held out her hand in her forthright way, and after a moment's surprised hesitation, he took it and shook it firmly. His expression clearly indicated that ladies who visited Bredon Stud didn't usually shake hands with grooms, head or otherwise.

"Pleased to meet you, Mr. McGuire."

"Pleased to make your acquaintance, miss." He shot a quick, curious look at Michael, which Michael blithely ignored.

"I'm giving Casey a guided tour. Want to come along and fill in all the odd bits of information I forget?"

"I'd be pleased to."

"All right. We'll begin with our pride and joy. Raj, our top stud."

Raj was a magnificent gray stallion. Tall and big-boned, he nevertheless had such perfect conformation that he looked graceful instead of awkward.

"What a beauty," Casey breathed.

"He's that all right," Dan commented proudly. "And 'e knows it, too. Conceited beast. You should see him look the mares over when they're brought in to him. For all the world like a sultan lookin' over a not very promisin' addition to his harem."

Casey laughed. Then she extended her hand palm up for Raj to sniff at. When he'd approved of her, she scratched his muzzle gently.

"Well, he's so gorgeous, I don't blame him for being conceited. I'll bet he runs like the wind."

"Very nearly," Michael said. "He won at Ascot two years ago. And at the Epsom Derby and Long-champs."

"And was promptly syndicated for a tidy sum and put out to stud," Dan spoke irritably. "It just kills me, it does. These horses are bred to run, but the minute they show how well they can do it, they're taken out of competition."

"A short racing career and a long sex life," Michael quipped. "It may disappoint people who like to see them run, myself included, but it makes sense financially."

"Well, it does precious little to make their offspring tough, if you ask me." Dan's face was set in a stubborn frown.

Casey felt no hesitation about jumping into the discussion. "I agree with you, Mr. McGuire. These horses were meant to run. It's a shame the way big-money interests have taken over and made syndication more important than racing."

"You're so right, miss. I was just tellin' Michael that yesterday. But 'e won't listen."

Michael grinned. "I suspect Raj won't listen, either. He leads an idyllic existence now, and all he had to do to earn it was run like hell for two years. Besides, when you can get twenty million pounds— or thirty million dollars—for syndicating a stallion, it doesn't make sense to risk it all by having him race. Those are remarkably fragile legs, actually. Break one, and it's all over."

"Still, I wish I could have seen this one race," Casey said wistfully.

"Well, we've got a two-year-old filly who looks promising. Raj's first offspring. We kept her for ourselves. She'll be racing at Newmarket next week. You'll have to come."

Casey was rather taken aback at the casual invitation. Michael's offhand manner suggested *of course* she would come. But a week was a long time. Who knew what might have happened between them by then.

She murmured something polite and evasive, then followed as Dan led them to the next stall.

While Casey was looking over the horse, a lovely

little filly, Dan whispered to Michael, "By any chance, is this the bit 'o fluff with the temper?"

Michael nodded.

"Humph," he snorted. "'Bout time you showed some good taste. Now *this* one, I'll wager, does more than just *look* good on a horse."

Michael laughed softly. But he was glad Dan approved of Casey. It confirmed his own first impression of her.

They continued on the tour, and an hour passed pleasantly. Then, as they were heading back to the Land Rover, a pickup pulled up, with a single horse trailer attached. Emblazoned on the side of the trailer was the Dubai Stud logo.

A Mercedes pulled up behind the pickup and a man got out. He was young, no more than thirty, and attractive in a heavyset way. He wore an impeccably cut three-piece suit. Only his dark coloring betrayed his nationality.

"It's that ruddy foreigner come for the filly," Dan whispered.

Michael gave him a quick, disapproving glance, then moved forward to greet the man.

"Hamdan, good to see you again."

"Good to see you, too, old man."

To Casey's surprise, the man's accent was pure Oxford University.

"By the way, may I introduce Casey Cantrell, Hamdan al Dubai."

Casey murmured a polite hello. To her chagrin, Dubai took her hand, held it for a long moment, then kissed it, all the while keeping his gaze locked with hers.

"It is my very great pleasure, Miss Cantrell."

Then, to Casey's relief, he turned back to Michael. "I've come for that wonderful filly. My trainer can hardly wait to get his hands on her."

"Why don't you tell your man to get her loaded while we have a drink inside?"

"Thank you. I'll do that."

While he went over to the man driving the pickup, Michael turned to Dan. "You'd better help."

Dan looked sour but said nothing; he left, muttering under his breath.

Then Michael, Casey and Dubai went into the office. It was a comfortable, wood-paneled room with leather chairs and sofas and elegant little prints of thoroughbreds on the walls. Tea and coffee were laid out on an ancient oak sideboard against one wall.

Michael poured coffee for Dubai and Casey, and tea for himself. Then they all sat down.

Dubai smiled. "Ah, your people are prepared, as always. How did they know just when to brew this delicious coffee?"

"I asked the cook to have it ready about now."

"Well, it's perfect." Turning to Casey, Dubai asked, "Are you involved with thoroughbreds, Miss Cantrell?"

"No, I'm afraid not. I just admire them."

"Ah, as do we all."

"You're doing more than merely admiring them," Michael interjected. "You're building a really fine farm, Hamdan."

Dubai shrugged slightly. "All it takes is money. A very great deal of it."

"Well, the money you're putting into the field is warming the hearts of breeders, agents, trainers and managers."

"As I'm well aware. You know, throughout history, money could never buy health, happiness, love or a classic winner. Fortunately, I don't have to count the cost of failure. At least not yet."

Casey laughed along with Michael. Dubai was surprisingly likable, not at all what she had imagined a wealthy business tycoon to be like.

After they had talked for several more minutes, he said, "I really must be going now. I'm anxious to get my new possession home."

As they all rose together he turned to Casey. "Miss Cantrell, I've enjoyed making your acquaintance tremendously. You know, I'm having a party this evening. I realize it's shockingly short notice, but if you're free, I would count it a great honor if you would attend."

Casey had no idea what to say. Dubai was pleasant, but she didn't really know him well enough to accept such an invitation. Besides, she suspected this would be a very formal event—even at home she had nothing appropriate to wear.

When she hesitated, wondering how to refuse politely, he added, "Michael is coming. So you see, you will know someone. It won't be one of those horrible affairs where everyone is a stranger."

Michael gave Casey a shrewd look that suggested he understood at least part of her reluctance.

She said slowly, "I'm afraid I . . . that is, I'm not sure if I'm free."

"Please consider it. If you're free, I would love to see you. Good-bye, Miss Cantrell, Michael."

They walked outside with him and remained standing near each other as he drove off.

When he was gone Michael said quietly, "Hamdan throws quite a party. At his last one there were hot-air balloon rides and fireworks. And the champagne flows like . . . well, like champagne."

It sounded marvelous, almost like a fantasy. Certainly unlike anything she would do in Morrow, Kentucky. Still, clothes were a problem. Would her green velvet be dressy enough? Immediately she recalled Michael's criticism of it and knew she would never again feel quite attractive in that dress.

"I don't think I have anything appropriate to wear. I wasn't expecting an invitation like this when I came to England."

Michael cocked his head to one side and eyed her curiously. "Why *did* you come to England, Casey?"

"Why do millions of American tourists come?" she countered.

"I imagine each has his reasons. What's yours?"

"Why do you ask?"

"If you answer one more of my questions with a question, I will be forced to forget the good manners my nanny drummed into me."

"You ask entirely too many questions. I feel like a suspect being grilled by the police."

It was the truth, and he realized it.

"All right," he said, pulling back. "Forget it. Will you go to Hamdan's party with me tonight?"

"You have a habit of suddenly changing the subject that is very disconcerting."

"Good. I'm glad I disconcert you. You do a good deal more than that to me."

Though his expression was the same, the muscles at the side of his mouth had tensed, revealing he wasn't quite as nonchalant as he appeared.

Before Casey could think of a response, he repeated, "Will you go to the party with me?"

There were several very good reasons why she should refuse, but there remained a good reason why she should go: the same reason that had brought her here today. She needed to find out more about Richard Bredon. And so far, Michael was her best—in fact, her only—lead.

She looked away. "All right," she whispered.

She felt, rather than saw, his mixture of surprise and relief at her abrupt capitulation.

"All right," he echoed. "I'll pick you up at seven. And now I'd better get you back to town."

On the ride back, both Michael and Casey were silent. Casey knew what prompted her own silence; she wondered what prompted Michael's. And she wondered what exactly would happen that night. Somehow she doubted Michael would leave her at her door as he had done the night before.

At six o'clock that evening Casey was busy filing her nails when there was a knock at her door. It was much too early for Michael, and the hotel didn't have room service. Who on earth could it be?

When she opened the door she found a teenaged boy standing outside holding a large, foil-wrapped package.

"Are you Miss Cantrell?" he asked in a thick accent.

"Yes."

He held out a piece of paper and a pen. "Sign 'ere, please."

"But what for?"

"For this 'ere package, miss."

"But I didn't order anything."

He frowned impatiently. "All I know is, I'm

supposed to deliver this to you. An' I'm supposed to be off work now. So could you sign, please, miss?"

"But where's it from?"

"I dunno. I just work for a delivery service. *Please,* miss."

"All right." She signed her name and accepted the package. Clearly relieved, the boy hurried off.

Sitting down on her bed, she placed the package on her lap and unwrapped it. Underneath the gold foil was a white box with the logo *Trifles* and beneath it in smaller type an address in Knightsbridge.

Pulling off the lid, she found tissue paper. On top of it was a card. Written in a bold scrawl was "Please accept this in the spirit with which it is given. In other words, don't be all injured pride. It would give me very great pleasure to see you in it."

It was signed simply "Michael."

Parting the tissue paper, Casey found sequins glinting back at her on a carefully folded dress. Unfolding it, she discovered that it was a slinky, bias-cut black silk jersey. The sequins she'd first noticed were in a sunburst over the bodice and hips. The sleeves were long and close-fitting, the neckline high. Yet the dress was anything but demure. A thigh-high slit would reveal plenty of leg—and the fabric, Casey was sure, would cling to every curve.

It was a subtly spectacular dress, exactly the sort she would have chosen for herself if she'd had the money. She'd never worn an evening gown in her life. Even when she went to her high school prom, her dress was knee-length and not very formal.

But *this* . . . She held it up to her and looked in the small mirror. Michael had been right when he'd said she should wear something that would contrast with her hair and skin. Against the black fabric her skin looked almost luminous, and her hair shone as it had never done before.

The fabric felt almost sensuous to her touch. Oh, how she would love to feel it against her bare skin.

She sighed heavily as reality intruded. This was an extravagant gift, one she shouldn't accept. It would obligate her to Michael.

Immediately she dismissed the thought as unfair. Michael wasn't the sort to demand payment for a gift. Besides, he'd made it clear he was attracted to her sexually and intended to do something about it at the appropriate time. Whether or not she accepted his gift was beside the point.

However, there was a moral point involved she couldn't dismiss so easily. She was using him to get information about his father. As it was, she didn't enjoy misleading him. Under the circumstances, how could she accept a gift from him?

Laying the dress carefully on the bed, she sat down and read his note again. The line "It would give me very great pleasure to see you in it" affected her profoundly. She felt a shiver ripple across her skin just thinking about how she would look to him in this dress.

She looked at the clock on her bedside table. Six-twenty. She didn't have much time. What was she to do?

Then an idea came to her. She would accept the dress, but she would pay Michael for it. Not immediately, perhaps, since she suspected the cost was beyond her limited budget. But eventually, even if she had to make a series of small payments. This way, the money he'd put out on the dress was in the nature of a loan. It allowed her to look nice for the party.

If he refused, as she anticipated he would, she would tell him she wouldn't accept the dress. That, she hoped, would stop his protest.

Feeling much better, she slipped out of her robe and put on the gorgeous gown. It did indeed mold itself to her every curve. It was even sexier on than she had imagined it would be. She had known there was no way she could wear a bra or panties under it, since the lines would show against the thin fabric. Now, as she turned around to view herself in the mirror, she felt the smooth fabric cool and soft against her skin.

She slipped on panty hose and the black slingback pumps she'd worn with her velvet dress. The dress really called for more formal shoes, but these were all she had and would have to do.

Looking in the mirror again, she decided her hair didn't look quite right. Twisting it into a knot on top of her head, she eyed the effect critically. With curly tendrils escaping around her forehead and cheeks, it had a sort of Gibson girl effect that was just right.

Taking hairpins out of a bag in her suitcase, she pinned her hair in place, then put on the pearl stud earrings that had been her parents' gift to her at high school graduation.

There was a knock at the door. Her watch showed seven o'clock, and Casey knew it was Michael. Feeling flushed and excited, she crossed the room and opened the door.

He wore a black dinner jacket and matching slacks, and a frilled white shirt. His golden hair contrasted vividly with the dark suit, and his turquoise eyes looked even more piercingly blue than usual. As he took in the dress, her upswept hair and the glow of excitement on her face, his eyes widened with gratified surprise.

So, she thought with sly humor, he hadn't been at all sure she would accept his gift.

"I'm glad," he said simply. Then, after a moment, he added, "I thought it would look good on you, but I didn't expect *this*."

His look, as he took in her full, firm breasts outlined against the black silk jersey, was frank with desire. Her humor disappeared in an instant, and something odd seemed to have happened to her breathing. Belatedly she realized she'd actually stopped breathing for a moment under the impact of that penetrating gaze.

As she took a deep breath to steady herself, her breasts rose and fell. His eyes followed the movement and narrowed with desire. In a moment, Casey knew, there would be no question of going to the party, for they would be in each other's arms. And the magnificent gown, which he'd gone to such expense to provide and which she'd agonized over accepting, would be stripped from her as carelessly as if it were cheap cotton.

"I have to tell you," she began in a tremulous voice, "that while I appreciate your generosity, I insist on paying you back."

"No."

His tone brooked no argument, but she ignored it.

"The dress is . . . lovely, and I'm grateful to you for providing it, since I'll feel more at ease at the party in it. But it's too extravagant a gift."

He shook his head. "The cost doesn't matter a damn."

"Not to you, perhaps, but it does to me. I insist on paying you back as soon as I possibly can."

He was annoyed now. "I don't want your money, Casey. Can't you accept a gift graciously?"

"No. Not when it's this expensive and is from someone I've only known two days."

"There are no strings attached, if that's what you're thinking. Damn it, I don't go around bribing women for their sexual favors."

"I'm sure you don't have to," she said with more frankness than she'd intended. "But the fact remains that I would feel much better if you would let me pay for it."

"*I* would feel better if you would forget the whole thing," he snapped.

"In this instance, I think my feelings are more important than yours. Can't you understand?"

"No."

"Well, try. Because if you won't let me repay you, I won't accept the dress."

"You mean you'd return it now, after seeing how perfect it is on you?"

She felt a stab of regret at the thought of taking off the beautiful gown and putting it back in the box. But that was precisely what she would have to do, she knew.

She nodded. "Yes."

Before he could argue further, she went on, "If you'll send me the receipt, I'll reimburse you as soon as possible. It may take a while . . ."

"Good. Hopefully, before you get around to paying me back for it, you'll realize how silly you're being."

"Then you'll send me the receipt?"

"Yes."

"Tomorrow?"

He frowned. "Very well. Tomorrow."

She sighed with relief: It was over. "Okay." She picked up her small black evening bag. "Let's go."

As he opened the door for her, he said with a semblance of his old good humor, "Casey Cantrell, you are a very stubborn and proud woman."

"Well, stubbornness and pride are two qualities you seem to know a good deal about from personal experience," she returned with a wry smile.

The anger left his expression completely as he laughed.

They arrived at Dubai's palatial estate just outside London an hour later. It was an old Tudor mansion set in lavishly manicured grounds. Huge, with at least a hundred rooms, Casey guessed, it was awesome. Yet somehow, she thought, Bredon Hall was more quietly impressive.

As Michael had promised, the party was magnificent. Dubai had hired a small circus for the evening. In the center of his broad back lawn, which swept down to a man-made lake, an elephant performed tricks. Clowns juggled and did pratfalls, while highwire artists performed above them.

Hundreds of guests mingled on the lawn, standing near bonfires to keep warm, or circulated inside the downstairs rooms of the house. The guests were all dressed to the teeth in rich silks and brocades, furs and jewels. Ermine, fox and mink shone beneath the strings of lanterns that lit the area, and the soft lights reflected off diamonds, emeralds and rubies.

Casey was even more grateful to Michael now. If she'd shown up in this glittering throng in her simple little velvet dress from Lilly's Dress Shoppe in

Morrow, she'd have felt conspicuous. As it was, she knew she wasn't on the same social or financial level as these people. But they didn't know it, and that made all the difference.

The only other time in her life when she'd attended a high society affair like this had been with Jamison. Then she'd felt awkward and out of place, all too aware that the other guests were used to hobnobbing with each other at similar social functions, while she was an outsider. Tonight, however, it didn't matter who she was. Class might be the last dirty secret in America, as her father had commented when Jamison had dumped her so abruptly in favor of someone more "suitable"; but in England, it was a problem only for the English.

She, Casey Cantrell, was as good as the best of them, she told herself. Some of these people might suspect, as Richard Bredon's receptionist had, that she hadn't been born to wealth. But they couldn't be sure—and therefore, they couldn't snub her.

Michael accepted two glasses of champagne from a passing waiter and handed one to Casey.

"Cheers," he said, touching his glass to hers.

She smiled, then sipped the golden, bubbly liquid. It was delicious, but potent. She'd have to remember not to drink too much.

"Cold?" Michael asked.

"A little."

"Let's go inside. I want to say hello to our host, anyway."

They crossed a broad stone terrace and passed through open French doors to a ballroom packed with people. At one end, a small orchestra played dance music. Swaying couples moved languidly in

front of the orchestra dais. At the other end of the
room, tables covered with pristine white clothes held
silver trays and bowls filled with food.

Casey's eyes lit up at the sight of lobster, shrimp,
pâté, hors d'oeuvres, prime rib and other delicacies.

"Hungry?"

"Starved. I want a little of everything."

Michael laughed. "How can you pack so much
food into such a tiny body?"

She grinned. "It's just my metabolism, I guess.
Let's eat."

"All right. I'll feed you before you faint. Then
we'll set off in search of Hamdan."

Half an hour later they had emptied two heaping
plates filled with food and drunk more champagne.

"I think I'd better get up and move about while
I'm still capable of doing it," Casey said with a smile.

"All right. Let's dance." Michael stood up, then
took her hand and pulled her up.

"I'm not a very good dancer," Casey protested as
he led her to the dance floor.

Taking her into his arms, he said huskily, "It
doesn't matter."

He was right: it didn't. All that mattered was that
their bodies were close, touching, separated only by
a thin layer of clothing. His hand pressed gently
against her waist; his other hand held hers possessively. Giving in to the warmth seeping through her,
Casey leaned her cheek against his chest and felt his
lips lightly brush the top of her head.

As they swayed together to a slow, romantic tune
from the thirties, the words vaguely flitted through
Michael's mind. "There's a somebody I'm longing to
see, I hope that he turns out to be someone to watch
over me . . ."

He would like to watch over Casey. She was so small and fragile. For all her stubborn self-reliance, she needed a man to keep her safe and protected. A man to cherish her. A man to bring out all the passion she kept such a tight rein on.

Him.

Michael felt her breasts against his chest. The thin material of her dress did little to hide them. Desire shot deep into his abdomen as he imagined the body that was outlined so enticingly by that dress.

When would they make love? he wondered. Tonight? The thought intensified his desire. But tonight was too soon, he knew. He hadn't learned enough about her yet; didn't understand her fears and hopes and needs. Before he could discover her body, he would have to take the time to know her mind and free her heart. That would make their lovemaking all the more passionate.

He felt a quick flash of humor at the thought that he was taking such care with this woman. Patience wasn't normally one of his virtues. When he saw a woman he wanted, he pursued her and as quickly as possible satisfied his desire for her. He saw to it that the woman was thoroughly satisfied as well— physically, at least.

But now he wanted more than that, much more. It suddenly occurred to him that what he really wanted was for Casey to care about him, a sobering thought to a man who generally considered himself incapable of needing anyone.

The song ended. For a moment Casey and Michael remained in each other's arms. Then Casey looked up at him. Her tawny eyes were dark with passion and her full bottom lip trembled slightly.

Tonight . . . he could have her tonight, could feel

her body beneath his, could take her to ecstasy and beyond.

It was all he could do to control his need for her. Letting go of her hand, he stepped back and took a ragged breath.

"We'd better go find Hamdan now." His voice sounded unfamiliar to his own ears, as if it belonged to someone else. Someone not nearly as in control as Michael Bredon normally was.

She nodded but didn't speak.

As they made their way through the crowd on the dance floor and into an adjoining sitting room, Casey felt giddy. And she knew very well it wasn't from what little champagne she'd drunk.

When Michael had taken her into his arms, it had felt like the most natural thing in the world. She wasn't a good dancer, but her awkwardness had seemed to disappear as she'd stepped into his embrace. All her nervousness, the defensiveness she'd felt with men ever since Jamison, had dissolved. Her body had moved with Michael's as if they'd been meant to go together, two halves of one whole. Even the song had contributed to the romantic feelings sweeping over her. It was her favorite old song, one she remembered her mother singing in a surprisingly good voice.

Her determination to take care of herself, her refusal to let herself be vulnerable—all the safeguards against *feeling* that she'd thought operated automatically to protect her—had faded in Michael's arms, replaced by a profound sense of safety and reassurance and belonging. It was at once incredibly sweet and rather terrifying. She'd only known him two days, and already he made what she'd felt for Jamison seem shallow and unimportant.

As they made their way through the crowd, Michael smiled and nodded at various people. But he didn't stop to talk, and Casey was glad. She didn't feel like making small talk with strangers at the moment. Her mind was too caught up in trying to sort out these strange new emotions flooding through her.

"Ah, there's Hamdan," Michael said.

Looking up, Casey saw Dubai standing in a corner, talking to another man whose back was turned to them. They made their way over to the two men, and Michael said politely, "Great party, Hamdan. As usual. You spoil everyone terribly."

Hamdan smiled broadly, clearly delighted by the compliment. "Miss Cantrell, I'm so glad you could come. I hope you're enjoying the party as well."

She started to answer that it was wonderful when suddenly she recognized the man who'd been talking to Dubai.

Richard Bredon.

Fortunately Michael didn't seem to notice that she choked on the words, for he had turned to his father. "I didn't expect to see you here. You normally avoid parties like the plague."

His father didn't respond to the teasing. He was too busy staring at Casey.

Michael went on, "By the way, Father, this is Miss Casey Cantrell. Casey—"

"We've met." Richard's words were curt to the point of rudeness.

Michael realized immediately that something was wrong. But Hamdan didn't.

"Good," he said, "you already know each other. See, Miss Cantrell, I assured you that you wouldn't be surrounded by strangers tonight. I—"

He was interrupted by a servant, who whispered something to him in a very low voice.

"Very well," Hamdan said with a long sigh, "I'll take care of it immediately." Turning back to his guests, he begged them to excuse him for a moment.

The instant he was gone Richard turned on Casey. "What are you doing here? And with my son?"

She opened her mouth to speak, but no words came.

Michael's gaze flashed from his father to Casey and back again. "What's going on here? How do you two know each other?"

Richard's expression was one of barely controlled fury. "This young woman came to see me two days ago. I threw her out."

"Threw her out! What the hell do you mean?" Michael was angry and confused.

Richard didn't answer his son. Instead he turned on Casey. "It was very clever of you to manage to get to know my son so quickly. Obviously, you're using him to get to me. But it won't work. I don't know what you're up to, young woman, but I'm beginning to suspect it's no good. What are you after—blackmail?"

"Of course not!" Casey had found her voice. For the moment, her anger at Bredon eclipsed her concern for what Michael would think.

Michael spoke through clenched teeth. "I want an explanation."

"The explanation's simple," his father answered. "You've been used by this . . . person. She came to see me, claiming I was involved with her mother. I threw her out. And she immediately scraped acquaintance with you. I'd advise you to send her packing, as I did."

There were so many things Casey wanted to say. Too many. Before she could organize her thoughts to speak, Bredon said, "I'll talk to you later, Michael," and left.

At that moment Hamdan returned, beaming happily. "Ah, Michael, Miss Cantrell. Sorry for the interruption—"

"Excuse us, Hamdan." Michael's tone was barely polite. He took Casey's wrist in a grip so hard it hurt and dragged her through the crowd.

"Let go of me!" she cried.

Without bothering to respond, he pulled her through the open French doors, across the terrace and onto the lawn. The circus performances were over now, and very few people were still out by the bonfires. Michael kept walking, dragging Casey behind him until he came to a small summer house. It was dark and empty. Roughly, he forced her inside.

In the shadows of the small dark room, he glared at her. Casey hadn't thought ahead to what would happen when he found out about her meeting with his father. But even if she had, she wouldn't have been prepared for his anger.

"What the hell is going on?"

She tried to steady herself so that she could reply coherently. "I did go to see your father, it's true. But everything else he said is wrong."

"Why did you go to see him?"

"It's kind of complicated . . ."

"Make it simple. I'm in no mood for an elaborate lie."

Now *she* was angry. "You might at least hear me out before you decide I'm a liar!"

"I'm hearing you out. That's why we're here instead of in my car headed back to your hotel room.

That is, assuming I would even have given you a ride back."

"Oh! You and your father are exactly alike, aren't you? You can't be bothered learning the truth."

His mouth twisted in a bitter expression. "Does your truth have a price, Miss Cantrell?"

She went rigid with a cold fury. "Are you accusing me of blackmail, too?"

"I'm not accusing you of anything—yet. What's your explanation?"

"I don't owe you an explanation. And you can forget the ride back to the hotel. I'll get a cab."

She turned to leave, but he caught her arm and whirled her around to face him.

"You're not going anywhere. Answer my question. Were you trying to blackmail my father?"

"I'm not answering your questions. Let me go!"

"Was he right? Were you using me to get to him?"

She was too hurt and angry to care what he thought any longer. "You Bredons obviously like to make up your own minds about people without giving them the benefit of the doubt. So think what you like. I don't care. Just let me go."

His blue eyes glinted quicksilver with anger. Shadows obscured his face, making him look rather frightening.

When he spoke, his voice was low and deadly. "I knew there was something going on. I just didn't know what."

Casey reached out to force his hand off hers, but he caught it with his other hand. Now he held her facing him.

"Now I understand why you came to Bredon Hall. And why you went out with me last night." His eyes narrowed in anger. "Just how far were you willing to go with me?"

Casey was profoundly hurt by the implication of his question—and furious at being held against her will.

He went on coldly, "I think you owe me something. And I demand payment *now*."

Thrusting her hands behind her back, he moved against her. His mouth came down on hers to savage it mercilessly.

For one split second Casey resisted. Her anger was a barrier between them, protecting her emotions from the onslaught of his lips. Then her senses were overpowered, and her anger dissolved in a rush of dark desire.

She fought not to feel those lips forcing hers apart, tried desperately not to respond to the moist warmth of his tongue sliding over her own. But her struggle only intensified the friction between them.

Her anger was lost, her will to resist was lost. Finally, she was completely lost in wanting him.

Chapter Five

Somewhere in the background were the muted, far-off sounds of music, laughter, talking. But in the summer house the only sounds were the ragged breathing of a man and a woman caught up by passion. Fire and ice shot through Casey's veins at the same time, setting every nerve ending atingle. How could anything so frightening be so sweet? she wondered before all thought was extinguished.

His lips moved roughly against hers, as if he were starving for her. His breath was warm and sweet on her cheek. Her lips parted completely to willingly let him enter.

A tremor shook his body. His hands, which had so tightly imprisoned hers, left their painful grip to span her back and pull her against his rigid chest. Her hands went to his shoulders, then his neck, and her fingers curled in his thick, straight hair.

Casey was lost in pure physical sensation, her body pounded by wave after wave of sensory perception. She felt the strength of his arms, smelled his intoxicating scent, tasted his hard lips and velvety-smooth tongue. He kissed her as if it were the ultimate punishment. Instead it was the ultimate pleasure.

His breath was hot and rasping. The sound fanned the fire blazing deep within her. She curled her fingers even more tightly in his hair, pulling his face down to hers, and pressed her breasts against his chest.

With a groan he pulled his lips reluctantly from hers and rained quick, hot kisses all over her face.

As Casey clung to him, long slumbering desire came fully awake within her. It had been so long . . . so very long since she'd felt this insatiable hunger, since she'd known this ecstatic explosion of urgent need and immediate gratification.

She felt like a top that had spun wildly out of control, whirling crazily, lost in dizzying sensations. Michael's hands were everywhere on her body now, searching, kneading, stroking. And everywhere they touched, her body came bursting to life.

He thrust his hands into her hair, undoing the loose knot and sending the bronze mane tumbling over her shoulders. His fingers dove into the lush hair, sending the strands cascading around her face and against his cheeks.

"Michael . . . oh, Michael," she murmured against his lips.

Her words were cut off by a renewed frenzy of kissing that left her breathless. Even with Jamison she'd never experienced such unleashed passion. The discovery of this deeper level of sensation impelled her to want even more from him.

"Please . . ." she whispered. She was begging not for release, but for fulfillment.

Then came the sound of voices in the distance, moving toward the summer house. The intrusion shattered the illusion of being lost in a world of their own. Michael came to his senses first; using every ounce of self-control, he pulled himself together.

For one eternal moment she gazed at him, profound disappointment etched on her soft, rounded face. What he saw in her golden-brown eyes touched him as nothing else ever had: she was bewildered, vulnerable, confused. He watched as shame washed over her and wished he could make that ugly emotion disappear.

She had nothing to be ashamed of. All she'd done was respond to his determined seduction in a way that had completely vanquished his anger toward her. Her startled pleasure in the feelings he'd elicited revealed her inexperience.

Bitterly he berated himself. He was older than she, infinitely more experienced, and should have been wiser. As well as kinder.

As the voices grew louder, Michael pulled Casey against him and held her trembling body in a tender embrace. When she stopped trembling he led her out of the summer house, keeping his arm around her protectively as they passed the couple whose voices they'd heard.

What came over me? Casey asked herself. She was shaken to her very core. Back in that summer house she'd discovered a whole new aspect to her personality . . . and it made her feel horribly embarrassed.

How could she have behaved with such wanton

abandon? But the answer was walking right next to her.

Michael.

She wanted him as she'd never imagined herself wanting any man—five minutes ago she would have let him strip her naked and take her on the dusty floor. The fact that they were in a fairly public place hadn't mattered one bit. Even when they'd heard other people approaching, Michael, not she, had been the first one to put a stop to their lovemaking.

Perversely, she turned her anger at herself on him. It was all his fault. He hadn't listened to her when she'd tried to explain. He'd refused to believe her, calling her a liar—and worse. Then he'd taken out his anger toward her in the cruelest way a man could.

Damn him, anyway, and his father as well.

She pulled away from him, shrugging off his arm, and quickened her pace. She wanted to get as far away from him as possible, as quickly as possible.

But he caught up with her as she was passing one of the bonfires and grabbed her hand.

"Casey, wait."

She spun around and faced him angrily. "Let me go! I never want to see you again!"

She'd intended to be strong and harsh. Instead, tears stung the corners of her eyes, and her voice shook from the evening's relentless barrage of intense emotions.

His turquoise eyes were vibrant with feeling. "I'm sorry. Oh, God, I'm so sorry."

All pretense of strength was gone now as tears streamed down her cheeks. "Just let me go . . . *please.*"

"I can't do that. I can't *ever* do that."

He pulled her into his arms and held her trembling body with infinite gentleness.

They stood silhouetted against the bonfire, a man and a woman embracing.

From the terrace, Richard looked out onto the lawn and saw them. He knew immediately who they were, yet in his mind's eye the two figures darkly outlined against the blazing fire took on a different shape. The other people strolling on the lawn faded from sight, as did the terrace, the mansion, the sounds of laughter and gaiety coming from within. The brisk October evening became a bitter cold night in late winter. And the figures silhouetted against the fire were he and Jesse. . . .

A week after their first meeting, he got another overnight leave. He went straight to the Montfort Theatre and watched Jesse perform. All week long he'd told himself he'd imagined the attraction he'd felt for her. That kind of instantaneous chemistry tended to weaken with prolonged contact. It was fantasy, and fantasy shattered easily.

Yet the moment he saw her again on the stage, he felt a surge of desire stronger than anything he'd ever felt in his life. She awakened in him everything he had thought dead—not just passion but other emotions as well. He wanted her in his bed as quickly as possible, wanted to engulf that tiny body in his larger one. But even more than that, he wanted to know her heart and mind.

She would be reluctant, he knew. It was probably too soon after the loss of her husband. But time was a luxury they didn't have. Each time he flew a mission, he was aware it could be his last.

At twenty-three he was already one of the older pilots.

They had to take what time they had *now,* for it might be all they would ever have.

When her performance was over, he left the theater and waited across the street, at Half-Moon Square.

He'd smoked half a dozen cigarettes, grinding the butts into the damp grass with the heel of his shoe, before she appeared. She came through the stage door in the narrow alley at the side of the theater. Pulling the collar of her tan trench coat up around her face to ward off the mist of the bitterly cold February night, she made her way across the crowded street to the square.

"Mrs. Cantrell!"

She stopped and turned toward him. As he walked up to her he saw surprise, then pleasure cross her face. But the pleasure was immediately replaced by a guarded expression.

"Lord Bredon." As before, the tone was gently mocking.

"I'm on leave tonight," he said as if that explained everything. When she simply raised one eyebrow questioningly, he went on in a manner much less polished than usual. "I thought . . . that is, I wanted to see you."

Why am I doing this so badly? he asked himself.

She gave him that disconcertingly direct look. "Why?"

"I beg your pardon, Mrs. Cantrell?"

"Why did you want to see me?"

"I'd like to buy you a drink."

"To tell you the truth, Lord Bredon, I don't really care for champagne."

He smiled dryly. "To tell you the truth, Mrs. Cantrell, neither do I. And please call me Richard."

At his smile, she softened. He's really very young, she thought. Younger than Frank was.

At that moment a couple passed them: an American soldier, barely out of his teens, and an English girl even younger. They made an oddly touching pair, he in his uniform with trousers that were just a bit too long, she in a cheap, brightly colored dress.

"C'mon, Ethel . . ."

"Edna."

"Right. *Edna.* I've only got tonight. I'm flying a mission tomorrow. Let's go back to your place."

"I don't know, Joe. It's late and we've only just met."

Her tone was uncertain. Clearly she wanted to be persuaded.

"Hey, sweetheart, how long does it take to get to know a person, anyway? You and me hit it off right off the bat, didn't we?"

As they walked on, their voices faded in the distance, his cajoling, hers weakening by the moment.

Jesse turned her golden-brown eyes on Richard, the expression in them wise beyond her twenty years.

"She'll let him come back to her place. And tomorrow he'll fly his mission. And *if* he returns from it, who knows? He may even call her again—if he can remember her name."

Richard's voice was quietly reassuring. "I didn't forget your name. And I'm not asking to go back to your place. I just want to talk to you for a little while."

She trembled, the first sign of a break in her defenses. "They're both just lonely and scared."

"Yes. We all are."

Seconds ticked by. Neither felt the bitter cold as they looked at each other. Then Jesse's sweet rosebud mouth curved in a smile that was no longer mocking, but gentle.

"I *would* like some coffee, Richard."

He felt as he did each time his plane touched down safely on the runway after a mission. "I'll buy you a cup of coffee, Mrs. Cantrell."

"Jesse."

His slate-blue eyes shone with a luminous intensity. *"Jesse."*

Later, at the Half-Moon Pub, they sat in a quiet corner, talking over coffee and tea.

"Tell me about yourself, Jesse."

She smiled. "What would you like to know?"

"Everything."

"Is that all? It might take a while."

"I've got all night."

Her smile faded and she gave him a sober look. "When do you fly again?"

"Tomorrow night, if the weather's clear. We fly at night and the Yanks fly during the day."

"Why?"

He shrugged. "Who knows? They just worked it out that way. Where are you from?"

"Kentucky. I grew up on a farm in the middle of nowhere. It's quite a change, being in a city like London."

Crossing his arms on the table, he leaned forward. "Do you like it?"

She considered the question for a moment.

"Well . . ." Looking up at him, she flashed a rueful smile. "To tell the truth, no. I miss the country. The quiet. The clean smell."

"I have a place in the country. I'll take you there."

"Emily told me about Bredon Hall. Quite grand, she said."

"I suppose it is. But it's quiet. And the air smells clean and fresh."

Suddenly they heard the sound of an ambulance siren outside.

He added, "There aren't any sirens there. No bombs dropping. No air raids."

She smiled again. "In that case, I'll go."

"What did you do in Kentucky?"

"Worked on the farm. I was the only child, and there was a lot to do."

"Did you like it?"

"I didn't mind it. On Saturday nights sometimes we'd have our neighbors over and everyone would play different instruments and sing. And I sang in the church choir."

Richard's eyes glinted mischievously. "Now you sing risqué little numbers at the Montfort Theatre in Piccadilly, London."

She returned his smile. "It is ironic, I suppose. But I wanted to come over here, and my voice was the means to do that."

"Will you return to the States now?"

"In two months, when this tour is over."

He was silent for a moment. Then he asked gently, "Do you mind talking about your husband?"

She shook her head. "No. In fact, there have been times when I wished I could talk to someone about him. None of the other girls in the troupe ever met him. Sometimes I'd read his letters to them, but that wasn't the same as meeting him, knowing what he was like and why I cared for him."

"Emily's pretty sympathetic. You could talk to her."

"Well, we haven't known each other very long. I guess the person I confide in most is Rose Donovan. She never met Frank, but her husband was in his Jedburgh Group with him. He was killed at the same time."

Richard's eyebrows rose in surprise. "I've heard about the Jedburgh Group—three-man teams, American, British and French, trained together to do top-secret work behind enemy lines. Frank must have been very special to get such duty."

Jesse's eyes misted with a tearful pride. "Yes, he was very special. We grew up together. Like you and Emily, I guess. I had a crush on him for as long as I could remember. He was reckless and charming, not like any of the other boys I knew. He thought I was just a pesky kid, always tagging along. Until one day . . ."

"He realized you weren't a kid anymore?"

She smiled. "Yes. When he was home on leave last year, we got married." Her smile faded slowly. "We had one week together."

"I'm sorry, Jesse."

"You shouldn't be. I'm not the only one who's gone through this."

Richard spoke slowly. "Last week, I had to notify a woman that her husband, who had been my tail gunner, was dead. He was nineteen. She's probably not even that old. Before we flew that mission, she'd called the base and left a message telling him she'd just learned she was pregnant. It made her feel better somehow to know that she still had part of him. And most important, that he knew part of him would live on."

Jesse's look was eloquent. "I understand. Oh, how I understand."

"But . . ." Richard stopped, then went on in an unsteady voice, "He never got the message, you see. He didn't know about his child when he died." He finished in a whisper, "I didn't tell her that. I couldn't take away the only comfort she had."

Her voice was heavy with sadness. "When is this horror going to end?"

He looked at her poignantly. "I don't know."

"I don't want to talk about the war anymore tonight. I don't even want to think about it, for a few hours, at least. Talk to me about something else. Anything else. Tell me about your family, Richard."

"There's only my mother left now. She lives at Bredon Hall and tends roses. My father loved to ride to hounds. He took a fence a bit too quickly a few years ago, and died. I suppose that was how he would have chosen to go."

"No brothers or sisters?"

He shook his head. "I had an older brother, Roger. He was my idol, really. Five years older, very dashing. Afraid of nothing. My mother always said he was our father all over again."

"What happened to Roger?"

Richard looked at her for a moment before answering. When he spoke, there was an odd mixture of bitter irony and irreparable loss in his voice. "He was killed fighting in France. I'm afraid, Jesse, we can't avoid talking about the war, no matter how hard we try. It's touched everything."

"Yes. I'm sorry about Roger."

"The strange thing was getting used to being Lord

Bredon. All my life I'd grown up with the knowledge that the title and all would go to Roger. He was prepared for it from the time he was small. My parents were always telling him what an important responsibility he would shoulder one day."

"You mean the house, the estate, whatever, would all go to him? It wasn't to be split between you?"

His lips curved in a humorless smile. "Clearly, you don't understand the English tradition of primogeniture. The estate was entailed."

"Weren't you envious?"

"Envious? No, definitely not. I didn't want the responsibility. I wanted to be free to pursue whatever life I chose. Roger knew from the beginning exactly what sort of life he would have to lead, whether he wanted to or not. He had no options, no freedom. No, I didn't envy him. At times I pitied him."

Jesse cocked her head to one side and eyed him thoughtfully. "And now, whether you wanted it or not, the responsibility's yours."

He managed a determined smile. "Yes, but I'm not going to let it force me to be something I don't want to be."

"And what is that?"

"Stuffy."

She laughed softly. "No. You're not stuffy."

She sparkled when she laughed, he thought. Her entire face lit up, her golden eyes reflecting the amusement in her upturned mouth. He would have to see to it that she laughed more often.

She went on, "According to Emily, you were something of the black sheep of the family. A bit wild and rebellious."

"Of course. It's a tradition in aristocratic families. The older son is responsible and the younger one a rakehell."

"And now the rakehell will have to turn all proper and well behaved." She grinned impishly.

"Perhaps. But not tonight."

The look in his eyes, the sudden huskiness in his voice, put her back on guard. She was reminded of that electrifying moment when their eyes had first met, the moment when she'd realized he was attracted to her. And more disturbing, that she was attracted to him.

"More coffee?" asked the barmaid in a thick Cockney accent.

Jesse nodded. "Yes, please." She didn't really want it, but it would give her something to do with her hands—and would prolong the moment when they would have to leave the pub.

"Tell me about Bredon Hall."

"It's relatively small by manor house standards. Queen Anne period. Rather lovely." He gave her a very direct look. "Suddenly, you're nervous."

"I'm not. Is your family wealthy or merely genteel?"

"Comfortable, I'd say. You *are* nervous, Jesse."

"My family was poor. Dirt poor, we call it in the States. But everyone else around us was, too, so I didn't feel it."

"Does it matter whether we're poor or rich?"

"Yes. We come from very different worlds, you see. I'm not the sort of person your mother would probably even want to receive."

"My mother has nothing to do with what's happening between us."

She looked away. "Nothing's happening between us."

Reaching out, he took her hands and held them between his on top of the small round table. At his touch her entire body went still.

"*Something's* happening between us. I've thought about you all week. Don't try to tell me you haven't thought of me."

She looked at him, anger flashing in her eyes. "I *haven't* thought of you." His fingers were gently kneading hers, creating ever-widening ripples of warmth deep within her. "I haven't," she finished weakly.

"Ten o'clock! Closin' time," a stentorian voice bellowed above the chatter of conversation and clink of glasses.

"I have to go." Jesse pulled her hands from Richard's. She rose and moved quickly toward the door.

Dropping some coins on the table for their coffee and tea, Richard followed her.

There were few people on the streets. Because of the blackout, not many lights were allowed, so people avoided going out at night if possible. In the middle of Half-Moon Square, Richard caught up with Jesse as she headed toward her flat.

"Wait!"

"No!"

"Jesse, I want to see you again."

She turned on him. "Why? Because I'm a lonely widow, easy prey?"

"It isn't that."

"Isn't it? You're Lord Richard Bredon and you have an ancestral estate and you'll marry someone like Emily someday. I'm not your kind, and we both know it. So why would you want to see me, unless it's to seduce me?"

For a moment he couldn't think of the right words to say. How could he explain to her what was happening within him when he didn't understand it himself?

Pain and anger warred in her eyes. "Go ahead, Richard, say the line. It's practically a broken record by now. 'I have to fly a mission tomorrow, sweetheart. Give a little comfort to a poor, brave soldier. Tonight may be all we have.'"

Suddenly the night was split by the harsh scream of an air raid siren.

"Oh, my God," Jesse whispered. "I must get home."

She turned and fled across the square.

"Jesse!"

He started to follow, to tell her they'd have to go into the nearest air raid shelter. But a man running out of the pub slammed into him, knocking him to the ground. By the time he got up, Jesse was across the square, running desperately in the direction of her flat.

He raced after her, pushing past terrified people hurrying toward air raid shelters. Then the bombs hit, bursting on all sides. Those in the distance fell with a long, low whistle, while the closer ones sounded like a train going into a station.

In a matter of seconds there were blazing buildings on either side of Richard: the whole of the night sky was lit up, as if it were suddenly dawn, and smoke from the burning buildings funneled upward. But on the street, where frightened people ran wildly about, there was red heat, sparks, flying cinders, the rumble of falling stone and the sharp whistle of distant bombs.

Air raid wardens and firemen appeared almost immediately, doing what they could amidst the destruction. Richard fought to make his way in the direction Jesse had run only moments earlier. He couldn't see her, but he knew she must be there somewhere.

Dear God, let her be alive, he prayed.

He saw the body of a woman wearing a tan trench coat lying on the sidewalk under some fallen bricks, and for one awful instant his heart stopped. Then adrenaline flowed through him and he raced through burning rubble to get to her.

He reached her at the same moment an air raid warden did. Together they pulled the woman from the rubble and gently turned her over.

It wasn't Jesse.

As the warden tended to the injured woman, Richard raced on, shouting for Jesse.

He was soaked with perspiration from the heat, and cinders were burning holes in his jacket. The wall of a building crumbled immediately behind him. One second slower and he'd have been buried. Still he looked ahead, searching for red hair and a tan trench coat.

Then, across the street, he saw a figure huddled down a flight of steps at the entrance to a basement flat. Dodging falling bricks and burning rubble, Richard crossed the street that was a no-man's-land now.

It was Jesse. She lay in a corner, curled in a tight ball, terrified and sobbing.

"Jesse! I'm here. It's all right, I'm here now."

She threw her arms around him and held on to

him for dear life, burying her face in his chest. While the bombs continued to fall around them, he held her, stroking her hair and murmuring words of reassurance. She couldn't hear what he was saying, but it didn't matter. All that mattered was that he was there.

Then, as suddenly as it had started, it stopped. The terrifying whistling sounds died out. There were no more bombs. There was only the sound of fire engines shooting water onto the flames and ambulances making their way through the devastated streets.

Still trembling violently, Jesse looked up at Richard. Her face was tearstained and darkened with smoke. Her golden-brown eyes were wide with remembered horror. But he thought her the most beautiful thing he'd ever seen.

"I want more than tonight," he whispered in a choked voice.

He bent his lips to hers and they kissed as only two people can who know they've come within a hairsbreadth of losing each other forever.

Chapter Six

$\mathcal{M}$ ichael led Casey into his apartment. It wasn't at all what she had expected. The building itself—a tall, narrow old Victorian structure in the Mayfair district —retained its original pink terra-cotta façade in the neo–French Renaissance style, all ornate molding and Gothic carving. But the apartment, which occupied the entire top floor, had obviously been completely renovated. It was open, one huge space partitioned off into smaller areas by fiberglass screens. Low, comfortable sofas and chairs in a neutral nubby cotton fabric were casual and inviting, while modern paintings and sculptures added bright splashes of color and bold design.

Casey gave Michael an appraising look. "You're very unexpected."

"You mean because I don't live amidst chintz and period pieces?" He shrugged. "There's enough of that at the hall."

He led her to a sofa. When they sat down, facing

each other, he took her hands in his. "I'm ready to listen now. I want to know everything—why you're in England, why you met with my father."

"Oh, Michael, it's a long, complicated story."

His lips curved in a tender smile. "I have all night. I'm not going anywhere. And I'm not letting you run away, either."

"There was a moment, there at Dubai's house, when I wanted desperately to run away from you. I tried. But you stopped me. And now . . ." She looked at him through eyes that no longer held even a hint of defensiveness. "Now, I can't run away from you."

"We need to talk about what happened in the summer house, Casey."

She looked away, embarrassed.

He went on tenderly, "Not now. Now there are other things that need to be cleared up. But later . . ."

He let his voice trail off. Casey understood what he meant. What had begun between them in the summer house would have to be finished, and soon; right now, however, she had a lot of explaining to do.

Marshaling her thoughts, she began, "I mentioned once that my father was in the war. He was stationed here in England, in fact. He was badly wounded and never recovered entirely. He spent the rest of his life in a wheelchair."

"I'm sorry."

"There's no need to be. He refused to feel self-pity, and wouldn't accept pity from others."

"He must have been an exceptional man."

"Oh, he was." Casey's face lit with pride and love. "I can't tell you how much I admired him. And my mother was devoted to him. They were very happy together."

Realizing she could no longer be entirely sure of that, she added doubtfully, "At least, they *seemed* to be."

"Until . . ." Michael prompted.

"He died two years ago. It was pretty rough on both my mother and me. Then, a month ago, my mother died."

Reaching out with one hand, Michael gently smoothed Casey's hair back from her tired, drawn face. "You've had a pretty hard time of it, haven't you?"

"I told myself I was lucky to have had them as long as I did. After all, I had wonderful parents who loved me, and whom I loved. A lot of people don't have that at all. I had it for twenty-eight years."

Michael's expression had grown sober and introspective. He repeated quietly, "A lot of people don't have that."

Then, looking at her, he asked, "But what does that have to do with my father? Did your father know him during the war?"

She shook her head helplessly. "I don't know. Somehow, I don't think so."

"Then how did you hear of my father?"

Casey sighed. This was the hard part. She had no idea how Michael would take it. After all, carried to its logical conclusion, it might mean her mother and his father had been involved in an affair.

She said slowly, "I was going through my mother's papers recently when I found an envelope. It was with the mortgage and insurance forms and all her financial papers, so I knew it must be important."

"What was inside?"

"A note, in my mother's handwriting, asking that the enclosed envelope be delivered to the person whose name was on it."

Seeing the sudden dawning understanding in Michael's eyes, Casey realized he knew what was coming. She finished simply, "Your father's name, and London, England, were the only words on the envelope."

"Did you open it?" he asked immediately.

"No. I thought about it, of course. I was terribly curious. But it wouldn't have been right."

"Casey, it may mean nothing at all."

"Nothing? It was an old envelope, yellow and wrinkled. And the ink was faded. Michael, she wrote that letter a long time ago, but didn't want it to be delivered until she was dead. Whatever is in it is important."

"I take it you tried to deliver it to my father."

"Oh, yes. He denied knowing my mother. Then he unceremoniously kicked me out."

"He might have been telling the truth. My father isn't a liar, Casey. He's almost priggishly honest. Honor is everything to him."

She'd expected him to take his father's side. In his place that was exactly what she would have done. And no amount of arguing would accomplish anything, except to drive them into opposing camps, each defending their respective parent.

But she didn't have to rely on argument. She had tangible proof.

Since her run-in with Richard Bredon, she hadn't worn the necklace. But she'd been reluctant to let it out of her sight, so she'd kept it with her. Now she took it out of a zippered compartment in her purse and held it up.

"My mother gave me this several years ago, Michael."

He took it in his hands and studied it silently for several seconds. Then, looking at her, he admitted, "It's the Bredon crest."

She nodded. "I know that now. My mother didn't tell me at the time. She simply said it was a family heirloom and was very valuable. She was right, of course."

His expression had altered. Now he wasn't so quick to dismiss what she was saying.

"You have no idea how she came to have this?"

"None."

"Of course, someone else could have given it to her. It didn't have to be my father."

Casey didn't respond. She didn't believe anyone else would have had that pendant, and she sensed that Michael didn't really believe so either.

For a moment he was silent, clearly thinking furiously. Then he spoke slowly. "There's a portrait of my grandmother at the hall. It was done when she was a young woman. I think she was wearing this pendant."

"I took it to a jeweler's once to be cleaned. He said it was eighteen-karat gold, very old and very valuable. And if your grandmother thought enough of it to wear it when her portrait was being done . . . well, something like that wouldn't be given away casually, would it?"

He met her look. "No, it wouldn't."

"I could have rationalized the letter somehow, Michael. But not the pendant, too. It seems to me that my mother must have known your father at some point."

"Was she ever in England?"

"Not as far as I know. She didn't actually say she'd never been here. But she never indicated she had. My father didn't talk about the war very often, but on the rare times when he did, she acted as if she'd remained in the States while he was fighting over here. And he never said anything to contradict the impression."

"My father got around a good bit during and after the war. Perhaps they met somewhere else."

"As far as I know, my mother never left the States. I don't think she even left Kentucky. And I certainly don't remember your father coming there."

"He didn't. He's never been to the States. Last year I tried to persuade him to go to Kentucky to look over some horses, but he refused. Said European stock was good enough. I remember he made some cryptic remark about never wanting to go to the States."

Suddenly Michael's eyes lit with excitement. "Casey, what if it was your father who was given the pendant? And then later gave it to your mother? After all, he was here during the war. He might very well have met my father."

"I've considered that possibility. But somehow it doesn't seem right."

"It's the only logical answer."

"But is it? Consider this—why would your father give mine a pendant? That's something a man gives to a woman. And besides, if my father had given it to her, my mother would have worn it."

"Not necessarily," Michael insisted.

"She would have. She wore everything my father gave her, whether she really liked it or not. She never wanted to hurt his feelings, even when he picked out some atrocious thing that was just awful on her."

"You can't be sure of that."

"Then answer me this—why did my mother write to your father? And more important, why did she wait until both she and my father were dead before the letter was to be delivered?"

Michael was silent. He had no answer, and neither did Casey.

Finally he asked, "Did you give my father the letter?"

"I tried to. He wouldn't accept it." She couldn't help adding with a tinge of remembered humiliation, "He shoved it into my hand and ordered me out of his office. As I recall, his exact words were, 'I don't want to see or hear from you again.'"

Before Michael could ask, she added, "There was certainly no question of attempted blackmail. All I wanted to do was hand over the letter to him."

"Then why did he make such a charge tonight?"

"He's *your* father, Michael. You tell me."

"It isn't like him to be rude. And it certainly isn't like him to make serious accusations that he knows aren't true. He must have misunderstood."

"I don't think he did."

"Did you say anything that could possibly—"

Anger flared within her. "*No,* I didn't."

Suddenly she wondered why on earth she was even bothering to explain all this to Michael. He didn't believe her. Grabbing her purse, she stood up.

"This is pointless. I'm going."

He rose and placed both hands on her shoulders.

The contact was electric. Instantly Casey was unable to move, was barely able to breathe. Michael's nearness, his towering presence, overwhelmed her.

"I'm sorry."

The whispered words came straight from his heart.

For a moment Casey closed her eyes, trying to get hold of herself. When she finally opened them, their expression was lost. "I know. I'm sorry, too."

"Sit down." As an afterthought, he softened the order with a less imperious, *"Please."*

She did as he asked and let her purse fall beside her.

He went on, "It's just so strange. I don't know what to make of it."

"You've no idea how strange it is. If you had known my mother—she was so . . . ordinary."

Michael's smile was dry. "Is anyone really ordinary? Everyone has drama in their lives somewhere."

"But she was . . ." Casey groped for words to describe her mother to Michael, who would never know her. "She was a farmer's wife. She was attractive, but not glamorous or sophisticated. Her interests were simple. She liked to sew and cook. She was . . ." She stopped, then finished inadequately, "My mother."

"She was a woman before she became your mother, Casey. You only knew her in one role. That doesn't mean that's all she was."

"Of course not, but . . ."

"I know, it's hard to view our parents as human beings with drives and emotions that have nothing to do with us. Especially when we're trying to picture them in some sort of romantic role."

He gave her a no-nonsense look. "After all, that's what we're really talking about here, isn't it? The possibility that my father and your mother were romantically involved."

"Yes. But it's so hard to picture, especially after meeting your father."

"Believe me, it's hard for me to picture as well. My father's . . . well, he's like your mother is to you. He's my father and that's how I see him. Rather stuffy, but nice. Not someone to have romantic intrigues with attractive Americans."

"Oh, Michael, I'm so stupid. It just occurred to me what I may be suggesting about your father."

"What do you mean?"

"How long have your parents been married?"

"Oh, that." He smiled. "I wasn't bothered by the thought that my father might have had an extramarital affair, if that's what's bothering you. In the first place, I simply refuse to believe he would do it. And in the second place, my parents' marriage really ended a long time ago. So it's not as if you're shattering an illusion or anything, if it's true."

"I'm glad you feel that way about it."

"To answer your question, they've been married thirty-nine years. I know because my mother became pregnant with me almost immediately after they were married. And I just turned thirty-eight. Actually, I always wondered if . . . ."

He didn't finish the thought, but Casey had a good idea what he'd been about to say. He wondered if his parents *had* to marry—and if that difficult beginning was responsible for the ultimate failure of the relationship.

"Oh, Michael, something's just occurred to me!"

"What?"

She looked thoroughly upset now. "If my mother and your father *were* involved, then it means my mother was unfaithful to my father."

"How can you be so certain of that?"

"My mother was nineteen when they were married. I know she hadn't left Kentucky up to that point. My grandmother told me once when I was a little girl that when my parents married, my mother left the county where she'd been born and raised for the first time in her life."

"Casey, this may all be just imagination. You don't know anything definite."

"That letter is definite. And that pendant is definite. They're both real, they exist. There has to be some explanation for them."

Michael said quickly, "The letter. Of course. You could read it—"

"*No.*"

"Damn it, Casey, why not? If my father won't accept it, what do you intend to do with it?"

She admitted reluctantly, "I don't know what to do with it."

"Then read it. Solve this mystery once and for all. You'll probably discover it's nothing like you're imagining."

"I can't do that."

"Why not?"

"I can't explain it. Not in words you'd understand, at any rate. It's a feeling I've got. My mother intended that letter for your father. If she'd wanted anyone else to read it, she wouldn't have sealed it so tightly."

"But she must have known you could easily tear the letter open."

"Yes, but she knew I wouldn't do that. Don't you

see, Michael? She trusted me. I can't betray that trust."

"I don't see it that way, Casey. You tried to follow her wishes, but you can't do as she asked. It's impossible because my father doesn't want the letter. So I believe you're justified in reading it."

"No."

There was a stubborn set to her chin that Michael was beginning to recognize. It meant she wasn't to be argued with. Suddenly he felt infuriated by the whole affair. He didn't like mysteries, and already this one was causing serious problems between him and Casey.

"Then, damn it, destroy it! Forget the letter ever existed. Whatever's in it is ancient history, anyway."

Casey's voice was level but determined. "I can't destroy it, Michael. And I certainly can't forget it. Somehow, I'm going to deliver it as she wished."

Michael's expression softened as his anger left him. He knew he'd been wrong to even suggest Casey do something she felt was dishonorable, especially something involving her mother. But he felt strongly that she shouldn't continue on with what might prove to be a wild goose chase.

His voice was quietly persuasive. "Put it aside, Casey. It would be for the best. It can't have anything to do with you."

"I can't be sure of that." Her golden eyes were troubled and confused.

"Whatever's in that letter belongs to the past. Let the past rest."

"And if it won't rest, Michael? What do we do then?"

He had no answer for that. Reluctantly he admitted, "I don't know."

He reached out to tenderly stroke her cheek. Immediately warmth flooded through her, melting her anger. Her hands had been clenched in her lap; now she pressed them against his chest and looked into his eyes.

"I can't go through the rest of my life not knowing what this was all about," she whispered. "And even more important, I can't feel that I let my mother down in the one thing she ever asked of me. I know it doesn't make any sense, but somehow I have a strong feeling that it's important I do as she wished. Don't you understand?"

He gathered her in his arms and pulled her closer. "I only understand that I want you. You challenge my mind and fire my blood. That's what matters, Casey. Not some letter in a faded envelope."

His face was so close now she could see the tiny lines at the corners of his mouth and a barely visible white scar on his temple. She could see the gentle flare of his nostrils as he breathed in her perfume and the transformation of his pupils as they darkened with desire.

Desire and reluctance commingled in a profound push-pull of emotion. She raised her hands to his chest to push him away but instead found herself gripping his shirt tightly.

His lips grazed hers teasingly. "Say you want me as much as I want you."

She shook her head. *"No."*

A smile hovered on his lips, his eyes warm. *"Yes."*

Then he was kissing her hungrily, as if he'd been waiting all evening to eat and now intended to feast. Casey's tongue met his in momentary resistance, then gave way to his teasing courtship dance.

The moment she responded to him he shuddered,

then his kisses turned wild and hot. He'd wanted her from the first moment he'd caught her in his arms as she'd fallen. As she'd lain on the ground half-beneath him, he'd felt a profound stirring of emotion unlike anything he'd felt with other women in years. Then tonight in the summer house, passion had exploded inside him with an urgency that had left him nearly unable to control himself.

Now they were alone in a very private place. She was in his arms and there was nothing to stop him from taking her. The knowledge that this time their intense attraction would be consummated sent flames of desire shooting through him, cutting off all thought and making his body tremble with anticipation.

But the sofa wasn't the place. Putting one arm under her shoulder and the other under her thighs, he lifted her up and moved toward the bedroom.

Casey's arms went around his neck. Now that his lips were no longer on hers, dizzying her with wave after wave of sensation, her mind was clear once more. And nervousness flooded through her.

"No, Michael, not yet. Later . . ."

He looked down at her with passion-darkened eyes. "Not later. *Now.*"

"But . . . I . . ." She struggled to think of a good excuse to put off making love with him. "I'm not ready." Her voice was weak and lacked conviction.

"You're ready, Casey. And so am I."

They were in his bedroom now. He crossed to a king-sized bed on a low white platform and lowered her gently. "This dress is stunning on you. But just now I think we can do without it."

In a deft movement he unzipped it and slipped it off her, sliding off her shoes at the same time. She lay naked beside him on the smooth, taupe-colored bedspread.

As he looked down at her, she saw in his lean face a hunger of such intensity that the nervousness she'd felt turned into real fear.

"No, Michael, please."

Immediately the hunger was softened by tenderness. "There's nothing to be afraid of, Casey. I won't take you anywhere you don't want to go." He leaned closer, his breath warm and soft on her face. "And I promise you, darling, I'll go as slow as you want."

Her eyes were wide with apprehension. But she was also eager and yearning. Beneath the burning glow of his turquoise eyes, apprehension gave way to desire.

He saw the capitulation and was touched by it.

Quickly he shed his own clothes. Casey watched, then looked away in embarrassment, and finally looked back at him again, unable to tear her eyes from his lean, muscled form. His body had a hard, thoroughly masculine grace, like that of a swimmer or runner. His chest was broad and smooth, but there was a thin line of golden hair that ran from his abdomen to the coarser thicket of hair below.

Looking at him, she felt something in her throat and realized belatedly it was her heart.

He lay down beside her. One hand cradled her round cheek and one fingertip traced the lines of her face. "You're so beautiful. You've touched me in a way I still can't believe." The timbre of his voice lowered. "I need you, Casey."

The admission of need was torn reluctantly from him. He didn't want to reveal his vulnerability, she realized; but he couldn't help it. The knowledge that she affected him that deeply went to her very heart.

"Oh, Michael, I need you, too."

The forefinger that had been tracing her features moved to her full lower lip. "Do you know you have the sexiest mouth I've ever seen? For two days all I've thought of is what it would taste like . . . feel like . . ."

Involuntarily her lips parted to allow his finger to enter. His fingertip met the moist tip of her velvety tongue. Slowly he began to slide his finger in and out of her mouth, keeping the tip inside. Casey's lips automatically began slowly sucking at Michael's finger. It had a slightly salty taste that was surprisingly nice—and the rough feel of it against her tender lips was highly erotic.

She bit down gently, worrying his finger with her teeth as her tongue wrapped moistly around it.

Michael groaned hoarsely and closed his eyes for a moment. The taut lines of his face melted. Seeing what she could do to him heightened her own excitement. Deep in her abdomen, liquid fire surged and eddied.

The tension that filled her now was sweet, not frightening, and carried with it the promise of unimaginable ecstasy. Her entire body craved his touch. Hesitantly, she took his finger from her mouth and placed his hand over her breast.

She whispered, "Touch me, Michael."

He smiled at her tenderly. "I will, sweetheart. I'll touch you here . . ." His hand circled her breast, then moved down to her stomach. "And here . . ." It moved lower, tracing the curve of hip. "And here . . ." It was between her legs, gently insistent. "And everywhere my hands go, my lips will follow."

He took a taut nipple between his teeth and teased it with exquisite gentleness. His supple tongue circled the pale pink aureoles and center buds. Casey moved restlessly beneath him, thoroughly unsettled by the wild, fluttering sensations flooding through her breasts.

Then his head moved lower, as he'd promised, his lips following the path already blazed by his expert hands. His tongue skimming across her abdomen was startling and delightful. Casey moaned low in her throat.

At the sound, Michael looked up at her and a rakish smile lit his face. "I told you I wouldn't take you anywhere you didn't want to go. And the journey's just begun."

It wasn't an idle boast. Casey had thought herself at the height of excitement. Now, as Michael's hands and lips roamed her body masterfully, she realized she was nowhere near the ultimate peak of excitement.

His fingertips, callused from riding, evoked responses within her that she'd never dreamed herself capable of. They were everywhere, searching out her most secret flesh, from the soles of her feet to the inside of her thighs. And everywhere they went, his lips followed, soft and warm and sweet.

Casey moaned and writhed helplessly beneath the onslaught of Michael's hands and mouth. Her fear was lost now, eclipsed by a desperate need to soothe the irresistible urge within her.

"Michael, make love to me now," she pleaded.

He chuckled softly. "I am, sweetheart."

"I need to feel you inside me."

Looking at her flushed face, hearing the pleading in her voice, it was all he could do not to take her immediately. His whole being strained to find fulfillment deep within her. But he sensed it wasn't yet time. She needed even more than he'd given her so far. He didn't understand the fear that had gripped her when he'd first begun to make love to her, but he did understand that every last vestige of that fear must be laid to rest before she could enjoy his lovemaking as thoroughly as he intended her to.

So he took a moment to steady his rising passion. He drank in the graceful curve of her throat and the soft fullness of her body. Finally his gaze lingered on the glossy bronze of her hair, spread out on the pillow in glorious disarray as he'd envisioned it the very first time he'd looked at her.

Lord, she was beautiful.

But what affected him even more than her sensual beauty was her warmth and tenderness. She was utterly and completely feminine. He felt he could lose himself within her softness and find there the solace he'd always sought and never found.

"Casey. My sweet, sweet Casey."

"Oh, Michael, I want you so."

The words affected him like none he'd ever heard before. Other women had found paradise in his arms, but only with this one did he feel a sense of fierce pride and tender responsibility.

"I want you, too," he responded thickly.

"Make me yours. *Now.*"

He eased himself onto her. Casey moaned softly at the exquisite pleasure of his possession. His golden skin shone with perspiration and his breathing was ragged with the effort of holding himself back until she was at breaking point.

"Move with me, darling," he whispered against her throat. "Let's finish the journey together."

She began to move, slowly at first, with an awkwardness that touched him. Then, as she gained confidence, she moved more quickly, urged on by his powerful thrusting movements. Their bodies were in tune in a way she had never dreamed possible. They melded together, becoming one.

Every nerve in her body was alive with an electricity that seemed to flow in one direction—deep inside her, to the very core of her being. As all that electricity converged, Casey sobbed for release. She clung to Michael as to a life raft in a churning sea, quivering with the force of her need for him.

Everything quickened—his thrusting, her responsive movements, their breathing—until suddenly it all exploded in wave after wave of ecstasy as they shuddered against each other.

There was utter stillness around them. For one long moment, Michael held her, stroking her hair and murmuring words of endearment. Lost in the aftermath of passion, Casey barely took in what he was saying; but she was filled with the sense that she had pleased him enormously.

Then he moved off her and covered them both with the bedclothes. It began to rain outside, a soft pitter-patter at first, then a downpour, loud and hard. But Casey was warm and content in bed with Michael. Snuggling next to him, she felt a deep satisfaction that made everything she'd ever felt before seem incomplete somehow.

"Happy?" Michael murmured.

"Oh, yes."

"So am I."

One arm was around her shoulder, the other lay across her breast. Idly he stroked its soft fullness in a movement meant to be loving rather than arousing. Casey felt a tiny tingle inside that was pleasurable without being urgent.

"Casey?"

"Yes?"

"Look at me, darling." She did as he asked and was surprised to see a serious look on his face. "What happened to hurt you so?"

Was it so obvious, then? she wondered. Or was Michael just especially perceptive? She was beginning to suspect that where he was concerned, she couldn't hope to have any secrets.

"It was a long time ago," she finally answered.

"But you haven't entirely recovered. I'm not prying. I don't want a list of your lovers complete with statistics. I'm far too jealous and possessive to want to hear any such thing. But whatever hurt you has made you resist opening up to me. And I want to understand why."

"I didn't think you were prying. It's just that it was rather humiliating."

"Ah," he murmured. "Yes, I see. It's the humiliations that stay with us. We can get over almost anything, even loss and pain. But humiliation we never forget."

She began slowly, "I was a late bloomer, I guess. I was so into horses and generally being a tomboy that I didn't date much. Boys seemed to look on me as a friend."

Michael smiled dryly. "The boys in Morrow, Kentucky, are fools, then."

Casey returned his smile. "Well, perhaps. At any rate, I didn't see what all the fuss was about. Until I met Jamison."

"Jamison? He sounds rather imposing."

"Oh, he was. Scion of an old Kentucky racing family. Very wealthy, very polished and devastatingly handsome."

Michael felt a stab of jealousy. But he'd asked for this and now he had to hear Casey out.

She went on, "I was twenty and pretty inexperienced. He was twenty-five and, as we say in Kentucky, hadn't just fallen off the turnip truck."

Michael chuckled, grateful for the comic relief that soothed his jealousy. "I take it you fell madly in love with this worldly young man."

"Madly. All he had to do was look at me and my knees turned to water. I was in love. At least, that's what it seemed like. And he told me that he was, too."

"What happened?"

"He never introduced me to his family. Then one day I discovered why. He was engaged to marry someone else. She was more 'suitable,' as Jamison put it. From a wealthy, socially prominent family, too."

"The young ass!"

Casey tried to keep her tone light. "My father once told me that class is the last dirty secret in America, and I've decided he was right. I didn't come from the right one to marry Jamison, but he told me there was no reason why we couldn't continue seeing each other, as long as we were discreet. I wasn't good enough to marry, you see, but I was good enough for . . . well, some things."

Michael rose up on one elbow and looked down at Casey with a fierce expression on his face. "Listen to me, Casey. You shouldn't have felt humiliated—he should have."

Casey fought back tears as she remembered the awful sense of shame that had washed over her. "I felt so stupid and so inadequate somehow. All I could think of, over and over again, was that I wasn't good enough and she was. After that I didn't care about being involved with anyone. I didn't want to risk losing what little pride I had left."

He knew no words to erase the memory of her humiliation, so he simply held her until her body, which had gone rigid, relaxed again. Reaching out, he turned off the light. "Go to sleep," he said quietly.

She sighed heavily, then closed her eyes. A great deal lay ahead of her, she knew. She would either have to persuade Michael's father to accept her mother's letter or, at least, solve the mystery of their relationship. But that would have to wait until tomorrow. Tonight she was in Michael's arms. And for the moment nothing else mattered.

Chapter Seven

Out of habit, Casey awoke with the sunrise. For a
moment she was disoriented, unsure of where she
was. And something was different . . . Then she
remembered where she was and what was different.
She was in Michael's bed. And the difference between this morning and all other mornings was that
she wasn't alone. Someone was sleeping beside her.

It was an odd feeling—someone else's body
pressed against hers, his arm resting possessively
across her breasts, his cheek slightly rough with
stubble against her shoulder.

Pulling back slightly, Casey contemplated Michael
as he slept. When he was totally relaxed as he was
now, he looked much younger than his thirty-eight
years. With those determined eyes hidden and the
wry mouth relaxed, she could see past the arrogant
façade to the vulnerability beneath. Remembering
the considerable physical strength he'd shown the
night before, it was strange now to think of him as
vulnerable.

He stirred and Casey held her breath. She was anxious not to wake him, yet she hoped he would wake soon of his own accord. She wondered what he would say when he did. She was sure it wasn't as unusual for him to wake up with someone else in his bed as it was for her. Would he remember whom he'd made love to the night before? Or had she faded into obscurity the moment the lovemaking was over?

It was awful not knowing if last night meant to him what it meant to her. Women and men were so different in some ways, especially when it came to lovemaking. What was a cataclysmic event for one was a momentary pleasure for the other.

A lock of golden hair had fallen across Michael's forehead and was brushing his eyelashes. Tentatively Casey reached out and brushed the hair aside. It was almost ridiculous that anything male should be so soft and fair.

Michael stirred again. Without opening his eyes, he felt for her with his hand and pulled her back down against him. His first word was a softly whispered, *"Casey."*

She couldn't help smiling. As he opened his eyes and looked at her, she admitted, "I wondered if you'd remember who I was."

He returned her smile lazily. "Oh, yes. In the course of a misspent life, I've learned that a gentleman's first responsibility is to remember in the morning whom he took to bed the night before. You are Casey and you are occasionally irritating but always stimulating. Incidentally, you have managed in three short days to turn my life inside out."

"We're even, then. Because you've certainly done the same to my life."

"Have I? Good. It's gratifying to know you're as affected by this as I am."

Remembering what she'd been thinking only a moment earlier about men not being as moved by lovemaking as women, Casey couldn't help smiling.

"And what's so funny, my little Yank?"

"Nothing. Just a little free-floating paranoia biting the dust."

"If you need reassurance, I know the surest way to provide it."

He was propped on one arm now, looking down at her. The sleepiness was entirely gone from those brilliant turquoise eyes; instead, passion began to glow softly in their depths.

Casey felt an answering response deep inside. Her voice was suddenly thick and husky. "This time, let me see to your pleasure, my lord. It's the least I can do."

One eyebrow rose quizzically. "*My lord.* You know, that's the first time I've found those words appealing."

Casey ran her fingertips lightly down his back, luxuriating in the feel of muscle and tendon and smooth skin. Cupping his hard, flat derriere in her hand, she thought how different it was from her own. Everything about him was different from her. He was hard where she was soft, all planes and angles and leashed power.

And they fit together. They fit perfectly together.

With an enthusiasm that more than made up for her lack of expertise, Casey explored Michael's body as he had explored hers the night before. She found the places where the slightest touch could elicit the most profound response. And long before she'd grown tired of the exploration, Michael had reached such a state of urgency that he took her with a frenzied passion that brought them both to flashpoint almost immediately. . . .

After a bath and a leisurely breakfast, Michael took Casey back to her hotel. He had some things to attend to at the farm but promised to pick her up at seven o'clock for dinner. Though neither mentioned her mother's letter, Casey knew it was very much on both their minds.

Tired from a long night during which she'd gotten little sleep, Casey changed out of the black gown and into a nightgown, then lay down on the bed to rest. Her thoughts immediately focused on Michael.

When she'd been involved with Jamison, she'd desired him with an intense, youthful passion. She had thought their lovemaking was everything it was supposed to be. But after being with Michael, she realized how naive she'd been. At twenty she had no concept of how profound desire could be. And as for Jamison's lovemaking . . . well, he'd talked about how experienced he was, had boasted of his ability to please a woman. The truth, Casey now realized, was that he was a selfish, clumsy lover who'd thought primarily of his own satisfaction and given very little thought to his partner's.

After more than seven years Casey suddenly found herself feeling sorry for the girl he'd married. And with that thought, she realized she'd finally put Jamison behind her forever.

Whatever happened between her and Michael, she would be forever grateful to him. He had awakened her in a way she'd never dreamed possible —had freed her from a prison forged initially by

Jamison's cruelty and kept locked year after year by her own determination never to be humiliated again.

Casey closed her eyes and remembered the night before. The sweetness, the wild abandon, the passionate ebb and flow of need and response to that need. Michael had coaxed and teased at first, then stroked and caressed her until she'd writhed with abandon. He had taken time and trouble to bring her to a fulfillment she wouldn't have known otherwise.

But as wonderful as it had been making love to him, there was still a problem. No matter how hard she tried to tell herself that Michael wasn't Jamison, she couldn't help fearing the same thing would happen with him. After all, the social gulf between them was even wider. After only a few days in England, Casey had seen that class remained a serious issue—especially for the aristocracy.

Someday Michael would be Lord Michael Bredon. Lady Casey didn't seem to fit.

Besides, she thought, punching her pillow irritably and turning over, what made her even think Michael was in love with her? They'd known each other three days. *Three* days. It was much too soon to talk of love. He certainly hadn't done so.

Michael Bredon was a highly eligible bachelor who probably had an endless succession of women chasing him eagerly. At thirty-eight he clearly didn't have a desire to settle down with any of them. Why should his feelings be any different toward Casey?

Swearing softly under her breath, Casey gave up trying to rest. Her mind was too much in turmoil. Putting on her robe, she took the papers out of her suitcase, sat down in the chair and went through them again.

Once more she stared at the faded, yellowing envelope with Richard Bredon's name on it. What was in it? She felt an overpowering urge to open the letter and read it. Michael's arguments from the night before were very persuasive. She'd tried to do as her mother had requested, but Richard Bredon wouldn't accept the letter. Under the circumstances, surely it would be all right to read it.

But it wasn't all right, and no matter how hard she tried she couldn't convince herself of it. Neither could she convince herself to forget it. She had a strong feeling that whatever was in the letter was important. If she turned her back on it, she knew it would haunt her for the rest of her life.

No, she would simply have to try harder to persuade Richard Bredon to accept the letter. The only question was whether or not Michael would help by talking with his father. Casey hadn't wanted to ask him to do so, because he clearly didn't think the letter was that important. But eventually, if she could think of no other way, she would do just that.

In the meantime, there was one concrete step she could take. In going through her mother's papers, she'd found an old telephone number and address book. Among the names in it was that of Rose Donovan of London. Casey was determined to find this Rose Donovan and question her.

She knew that Rose Donovan might have moved, might have changed her number to an unlisted one—might even have died. When she dialed the number, she was fully prepared for a recorded message. Instead a cheerful voice answered, "Hello?"

For a moment Casey was taken aback. She'd been

so prepared for failure that she hadn't planned what she wanted to say. Finally she asked, "Is this Rose Donovan?"

"Yes, speaking."

At last something had gone right.

Trying to sound calm and collected instead of nervous and hopeful, Casey began, "My name is Casey Cantrell. I believe you knew my mother, Jesse Cantrell."

"My God, Casey! What a delightful surprise! But you sound so close. You're not by any chance in town, are you?"

"Yes, I am."

"How marvelous! Is your mother with you?"

"No. I suppose you haven't heard. My mother died a month ago."

"Oh, my dear, I'm so sorry. I wish I'd known. Poor little Jesse . . ."

Her voice trailed off sadly, all the bright good humor gone from it.

Something about the way she'd said, "Poor little Jesse," struck Casey as unusual. There was a profound pity there, rather than simply a sense of loss.

Mrs. Donovan went on after a moment, "Did your mother give you my name?"

"No, I found it in an old address book of hers."

"And since you were in town, you decided to call? I'm glad you did. I would love to see you."

"Mrs. Donovan, I don't want to mislead you. I am in London on vacation, but I'm calling you for a reason."

She heard the sudden intake of breath on the other end of the line, and she sensed Rose Donovan waiting with intense curiosity. She'd hoped the woman would turn out to be someone who could help clear up the mystery. Now she was sure of it.

She continued, "When would it be convenient to see you?"

"I think we should meet as soon as possible. I'm free now, in fact. Would that suit you?"

"Yes. I'm rather anxious to talk to you about my mother."

"I understand." Her voice was gentle and compassionate. "It's been a very long while since I saw your mother. But she was a good friend. Someone I admired tremendously. I'll be most happy to talk to you about her and to tell you whatever I can."

Something about the last phrase seemed guarded. But Casey was determined not to be put off in her questions. If Rose Donovan knew something, she would have to be persuaded to share it.

After writing down directions to Mrs. Donovan's house, Casey quickly dressed, then caught a cab outside the hotel. Fifteen minutes later she was in Islington, the old London district where Mrs. Donovan's townhouse was. Islington was an area of tall, narrow townhouses packed tightly together, with few parks or even trees. The neighborhood appeared to be undergoing renovation, for many of the townhouses showed signs of new paint and repair. Mrs. Donovan's house was extremely attractive, with a windowbox filled with bright red geraniums and a front door painted a vivid blue.

Casey's heart beat a little faster as she knocked on the door. Fortunately, she didn't have to wait long: almost immediately the door was opened by a tall, slim woman with graying blond hair and faded, cornflower-blue eyes. She looked to be in her late sixties, but there was nothing "little old ladyish" about her. Her subtle, expertly applied makeup and sleek lavender silk dress with a startling fuchsia sash showed a style and flair that were ageless. In her youth, Casey thought, she had probably been stunning.

"Casey, my dear, come in. I hope you don't mind if I hug you, but I simply can't resist."

She enveloped Casey in a warm hug that immediately made Casey feel welcome. More than welcome —in a strange way, Casey felt as if she'd come home, in spite of the fact that Rose Donovan was a perfect stranger.

"Now you must call me Rose, and I'll go on calling you Casey, as I've already started doing. Come inside and sit down. My, what a cold, dreary day. We'll sit by the fire, which is always so cheery, I think, especially on a day like this."

As she rambled on in her friendly way, Rose led Casey into a sitting room. Bright yellow walls were covered with lovely Impressionist prints. Vases of flowers were everywhere. The overstuffed furniture looked incredibly comfortable. This was a charming, cheerful home and Casey felt at ease.

They sat down on a chintz-covered sofa facing a small fireplace. A coal fire burned brightly, exuding warmth and security. On a lovely old cherrywood table sat a beautiful silver tea service and two cups and saucers of blue Wedgwood china.

"I hope you're a tea drinker, my dear. I don't care for coffee, so I don't keep any about. And there wasn't time to run down to the store."

"I love tea," Casey assured her.

"Lemon or milk?" Rose asked as she filled the cups with the dark, steaming-hot tea.

"Lemon, please."

Rose handed her a cup and saucer. As Casey took a tentative sip, she discovered that the tea was much stronger than the kind she was used to at home. Now she understood why Rose had offered milk with it.

Catching Casey's rueful expression, Rose smiled. "It takes a bit of getting used to, I know. Your mother used to say black coffee was mild in comparison. I never could make a tea drinker out of her."

Casey put down her cup. "Rose, you're being so kind. I want to respond by being completely honest. I've come hoping you could give me some information."

Rose's smile slowly faded to a still friendly but more serious expression. "Yes. I understand. What do you want to know?"

"Was my mother ever in England?"

Rose seemed surprised by the question. "You mean, you don't even know . . ." She stopped, then took a long moment to consider the question. "Casey, I must ask—why did you come to England? It's not just for a vacation, is it?"

"I guess you have a right to know that, since I'm asking you questions in return." Briefly she related the story of finding the letter with Richard Bredon's name on it.

Rose's expression was very serious now, but she didn't seem at all surprised. "I see." After a pause she went on, "Did you deliver the letter?"

"I tried. He wouldn't accept it. He even denied ever knowing my mother. But I'm sure that was a lie."

Rose didn't respond to that. She waited expectantly, clearly wondering how much Casey knew.

Finally Casey continued, "Ever since I found the

letter, I've had a strong feeling that it's extremely important. And after meeting Richard Bredon, I sense there's some sort of mystery surrounding it."

"You could put it aside, try to forget about it."

Casey shook her head. "No. I can't do that."

Rose smiled tenderly. "No, I suppose you can't."

"I would always wonder, you see, what it was all about. And I would feel I'd let my mother down by not fulfilling her last request."

"I understand, child. I *do* understand. But you must understand that you're delving into the past, into something that is perhaps better left undisturbed."

"Let sleeping dogs lie?" Casey asked wryly.

"Precisely. Oh, I realize that when one is young and full of zeal as you are, that may sound rather cowardly. But as one grows older, one learns that discretion may be the better part of valor."

"Maybe. But I *have* to know, Rose."

Rose sighed. "I thought you'd feel that way."

"Will you answer my question, then? Was my mother ever in England?"

Rose took a sip of tea, then looked at Casey over the rim. She was clearly making a decision, and Casey felt a sudden sense of panic that Rose would choose not to answer her questions.

Finally, Rose said quietly, "Yes, your mother was in England. It was a long time ago, during the war. Long before you were born."

Casey breathed an inward sigh of relief. She'd suspected that if her mother and Richard Bredon had met, it must have been in England. It was reassuring to know she was right. But it was also disturbing in a way, for it confirmed her fear that her mother had known Bredon after she was married.

She couldn't bring herself to simply come right out and ask Rose if her mother had been involved in an extramarital affair. And she wasn't at all sure Rose would answer that particular question.

Instead she asked, "How did you know my mother?"

"My husband, John, served with your father. They were on a mission together when John was killed. Your father was wounded trying to save him."

"I'm sorry, Rose."

"You needn't be. It was all a very long time ago, and I've long since come to terms with it. That was a hard time for many people. A time of loss and terrible sacrifice."

"My father never told me exactly how he was wounded."

Rose smiled softly. "He probably didn't want to sound as if he were bragging. I never met him, but from what your mother told me, he was an extremely modest man. But the fact is, he was a hero, in every sense of the word."

She went on, "At any rate, that's how I met your mother. Our husbands suggested we get to know each other and we did."

"You mean she was in London?"

"Yes, she'd come over with a USO troupe. I was doing war relief work, mainly with children who'd been orphaned by the war. Your mother came to the orphanage to entertain several times."

Casey interrupted in surprise, "To entertain?"

"Yes. She was a singer. Didn't you know?"

Casey shook her head. "No. She and my father never really talked about the war at all. She didn't actually say so, but she gave me the distinct impression she'd remained in Kentucky while my father was over here. And he never said anything to the contrary."

"She was only here for a short time. She came to be closer to your father, though as it turned out, she didn't see him much. That is, not until he'd been wounded and was brought back here for a short time before returning to the States."

Casey tried to remember her mother ever showing any interest in singing. She'd sung bedtime lullabies to Casey . . . and hymns in church. But that was all. She hadn't sung around the house.

Casey said slowly, "It's hard to imagine my mother as an entertainer. She was so quiet and shy."

"Well, she was a very talented singer. She made quite a hit with the children. I went to see her perform with the USO troupe a few times, and she was marvelous. Audiences loved her."

"I wish she'd told me. Why did she and my father keep it a secret?"

Rose hesitated, then answered reluctantly, "As I said, that was a very hard, unhappy time. Perhaps they simply wanted to forget about it, to put it behind them."

"I think there's more to it than that. That letter has something to do with that time, doesn't it?"

"Casey, I haven't read it. I can't know for certain what's in it."

"But you have some idea?"

"I can't try to second-guess what your mother may or may not have written. We were out of touch for many years."

Casey recognized that Rose was adamant on the subject. However, there was something else she could ask. "Do you know Richard Bredon?"

"I've never met him. I used to know his wife, Emily, but that was during the war, before they were married."

"Rose, was my mother involved with him?"

Rose set down her teacup, then looked out the window at the gray, overcast day. She had an open countenance, much like Casey's, and it was easy to read the interplay of emotions going through her—reluctance, sadness, discomfort at being questioned about a subject she obviously didn't want to discuss. Casey felt uncomfortable pressing Rose so hard, but she *had* to know. And Rose was her only hope.

Finally Rose looked back at her and answered evasively, "I will only say this—your mother and Richard Bredon knew each other. But that was nearly forty years ago, Casey. Whatever was between them ended then."

Casey shook her head. "I don't think it did end, Rose. Otherwise, why did she write to him?"

Rose didn't have an answer for that.

Michael whistled happily as he leaned on the fence, watching the yearlings gambol in the pasture. Brisk, cold days like this always made them frisky. They arched their necks, lifted their tails and cantered about, occasionally breaking into a full gallop.

This was a particularly promising group—a bay colt that should bring a good price at the Newmarket sales in December and a lovely little sorrel filly that might do just as well. A fast lady was worth her price nowadays. There were an increasing number of lucrative races for fillies and mares, and more and more females were racing against the males, commanding top dollar at the sales, winning stakes or foaling winners.

But Michael's mind was only partly on the horses and their potential for profit. He was really thinking about an entirely different female.

Casey Cantrell.

From the beginning there'd been something different about the way he reacted to her. And last night . . . He stopped whistling and thought about last night.

She'd responded to his lovemaking with a kind of startled pleasure and quiet gratitude that told him far more than she probably realized about her ex-lover. Jamison, he thought sarcastically, turning the word into an epithet. The young fool. But the other man's ineptitude had worked to Michael's advantage. He was inordinately pleased to have been the one to introduce Casey to such pleasure.

He began whistling again.

"Ye're happy today, I see."

Michael smiled as Dan walked up to him. As always, the little man wore his jaunty red cap.

"It's a nice day," he said by way of explanation.

"Nice?" Dan snorted. "Cold as sin an' likely to rain any minute. You call that *nice?*"

"Well, perhaps I'm simply in a good mood."

"Countin' yer profit with this lot, are you?" Dan asked, gesturing toward the yearlings. "Don't be too hasty. Prices are down, y'know."

"I know. But I think one or two of these will do well."

"Humph! If the bleedin' foreigners pay out some o' their extortion money for 'em, maybe."

Michael smiled. "See, you're beginning to understand the value of the 'foreigners' getting involved in racing."

"I'm not sayin' that at all. Things was better when

the landed gentry ran things. Racing had more class then."

"Dan, you're an old snob."

"I am, and not ashamed to admit it." He sighed heavily, then continued philosophically, "Well, some things at least will never change. It still takes courage, an' heart, an' persistence to come from behind an' fight it out to the finish."

All qualities that Casey had, Michael thought.

After a momentary silence he asked, "Have you ever been in love, Dan?"

Dan grinned. "Many times."

"I mean truly in love."

"Ah, you mean where you contemplate matrimony."

Michael nodded.

"Well, now," Dan answered thoughtfully, "I'll tell you somethin' I've never told a livin' soul. I was engaged once."

Michael looked at him in surprise. "I thought you were a lifelong confirmed bachelor?"

"Not always. When I was young—younger than you—there was this girl. Lucy, her name was. Pretty name, isn't it? I've always been partial to it."

"What happened between you and Lucy?"

"The date was set. The Reverend Claxton had even read the banns in church."

"Don't tell me you got cold feet and left her standing at the altar?"

Dan frowned. "O' course not. That wouldn't be a gentlemanly thing to do, now, would it?"

"No."

"'Twas Lucy what changed her mind," Dan admitted with some embarrassment.

"Why?"

"She said I didn't love her enough. Said she realized she'd always come second to horses, with me. And she didn't intend to take second place behind a stupid animal. She up an' married a plumber an' had six kids." He finished doubtfully, "I s'pose she was happy."

Michael could tell that Dan still felt the loss even after all this time. "I'm sorry."

"Ah, well, it was me own fault. If I'd just told her that she mattered more to me than any dumb horse, she'd a' married me. But I let somethin' come between us, an' lost her because of it."

He gave Michael a penetrating look. "You want to be careful not to let somethin' that doesn't really matter come between you when you find the right person."

Something like an old letter, Michael thought soberly.

Shrugging off the past, Dan said, "By the way, I come to tell ye yer father's at home. He called an' wants to see you."

Michael's voice was harder than usual. "And I want to see him."

As he headed toward the hall he thought about the question he intended to ask his father.

Chapter Eight

As Michael entered the house through the kitchen, he found the housekeeper, Mrs. Rawlins, just sitting down to tea.

"Where's my father, Mrs. Rawlins?"

"In the study, sir. I just served tea in there."

"Thank you."

He strode on through the house until he came to the small, wood-paneled study. As he opened the door he saw his father pouring out a cup of tea.

"Ah, Michael, you're just in time." There was a bluff, hearty tone to his voice that struck a false note.

He's nervous, Michael thought. He had a pretty good idea why.

Sitting down in a leather armchair opposite his father, he began without preamble, "I talked to Casey Cantrell last night."

For an instant Richard stopped pouring milk into

his tea. Then he finished and added sugar. All the while he avoided Michael's gaze.

"Oh? How did you meet that young woman, may I ask?"

"We more or less ran into each other accidentally near here. *I* was the one who pursued the relationship, not she."

Richard looked as if he didn't believe that.

Feeling a growing impatience with his father, Michael went on, "She told me about the letter from her mother to you. And she showed me the pendant. It was Grandmother's, wasn't it?"

"Yes."

"Did you give it to her mother?"

Richard didn't answer at once. He took a sip of tea, then balanced the cup and saucer on his knee. Finally he looked up at Michael. "I don't like your tone. You've no business questioning me."

"Damn it, Father, you accused her of being a blackmailer! And for a moment, I believed you." Suddenly his anger left him. "We've never fought, you and I," he said poignantly.

With a pleading look, Richard replied, "I don't want to do so now."

"I must know. *Did* you know her mother?"

Still Richard hesitated. When he spoke it was in an injured tone of voice. "I can't believe you'd take a stranger's word against mine."

Michael looked at him steadily. "I don't think you've ever lied to me."

Instead of reacting angrily to the not very subtle accusation, Richard looked chagrined. After an uncomfortable silence he said tersely, "I knew Jesse Cantrell. I gave her the pendant."

"Then why wouldn't you accept her letter?"

"It was forty years ago when I knew her. *Forty* years. That's a very long time, Michael. I have no wish to dredge up the distant past."

"But—"

"I'm not obligated to accept the letter merely because she wished it," Richard interrupted angrily.

"That's true. But aren't you curious?"

"No."

"What harm would it do to accept it from Casey? You wouldn't even have to read it. . . ."

"No!" Richard snapped. "I told you. I'm not interested in it. And I won't be badgered by that girl."

"She's just trying to do as her mother wished."

"That's her problem, not mine."

Michael couldn't believe what he was hearing. For as long as he could remember, his father had never behaved in a discourteous manner. Richard felt the responsibility inherent in his social position very deeply. If something "wasn't done," he didn't do it.

Michael had always thought him rather stuffy, yet he'd admired him at the same time. It was this sense of honor, of the importance of correct behavior and impeccable manners, that had prevented Richard from getting a divorce. Of that Michael was certain. For he knew how abysmally unhappy his father had been with his mother.

Yet now this man who'd always behaved so admirably was being rude, even cruel, to a young woman who'd done him no harm, who certainly didn't deserve such treatment. Why?

"What was Jesse Cantrell to you?"

Richard looked at him sharply. "What do you mean?"

"I mean, were you lovers?"

"That is absolutely none of your affair, Michael."

Setting down his teacup, he rose and stood by the fire, his hands clasped behind his back in what Michael had always teasingly referred to as his "Lord Montgomery posture." Now there was nothing humorous about it.

Looking down at his son, he went on, "On the rare occasions when I've questioned the way you've handled your personal life, you've told me in no uncertain terms to mind my own business. Now I'm telling you to do the same."

"I'm not asking out of idle curiosity."

"No, you're asking because that girl put you up to it!"

Michael rose and faced him. "*That girl* has a name. It's Casey. Or Miss Cantrell, if you don't want to get personal."

Richard's expression altered slightly as he sensed the depth of Michael's feelings about Casey. "I see," he said slowly.

"She's a nice young woman, Father. She isn't after anything. Certainly not blackmail."

"How can you be so certain of that? You hardly know her."

"I know her. And I'm certain she's simply trying to deliver that letter as her mother asked."

"*You* may be certain of it, but I'm not. I don't wish to have anything to do with Casey Cantrell. There's no valid reason why I should have to do so."

"Perhaps you don't *have* to do so. But it would make Casey happy if you would at least accept the letter."

"That young woman's happiness or unhappiness is no concern of mine."

"It is *my* concern."

Richard looked long and hard at Michael. "I take it you're involved?"

Michael nodded.

Richard looked as if he were trying very hard to control his anger. "Well, you've been involved with a score of young women before. No doubt she won't be the last."

Michael couldn't help smiling wryly. "Up to now you've made it clear you wished I would settle down and provide a son and heir. Now you're against the idea."

"Well, you couldn't be seriously interested in her."

"Why not?"

Richard's expression was really concerned now. "Michael, you've only just met her. And she's . . ."

"What, Father? What is she?"

"She's not of your class."

"You and Mother were the same class. It didn't seem to ensure a happy marriage for either of you. It just made it a little too embarrassing to go traipsing through the divorce court."

"Michael!"

"It's the truth. We both know it."

"I can't believe we're having this ugly disagreement. All because of that girl."

"I told you, her name is Casey. And it's unfair to blame her for this argument."

"I don't want to discuss this any further, Michael." Richard sounded tired and unhappy.

Looking at him, at the lines in his face that seemed to have deepened overnight, Michael felt sorry for his father. He would have dropped the whole thing if he could. But Casey wouldn't accept that. For her sake, for the sake of their fragile new relationship, he had to get at the truth.

"You never answered my question, Father. What was Jesse Cantrell to you?"

For a moment he thought his father would refuse to answer. Then the look of obstinacy that had covered Richard's face throughout the argument dissolved, replaced by a look of bitterness such as Michael had never seen before.

Richard's voice was cold. "Jesse Cantrell was just another wartime affair. Women like her were common enough then."

"What do you mean, women like her?"

"She was no good. Period. I don't have to spell it out for you, do I?"

Michael didn't respond. Somehow, this wasn't what he'd expected. And it certainly wasn't something he could tell Casey.

Without having touched his tea, he turned and walked toward the door.

"Michael."

He stopped and faced his father.

Richard hesitated, then asked awkwardly, "You're not . . . that is, you can't be seriously interested in that . . . in Miss Cantrell?"

"Yes, I am."

"But you've only just met, you know nothing about her."

"I know enough to realize she's completely different from the overbred, shallow women you've thrown at me for years. She's like a breath of fresh air. Yes, I'm seriously interested in her."

With that, he turned and walked out.

Richard sat down heavily on the sofa and closed his eyes for a moment. He'd handled it badly, he knew. Very badly. He should have denied knowing Jesse and left it at that. But Michael was right—he never could lie to his son.

The worst of it was Michael's admission that he was seriously interested in Casey Cantrell. Actually, he didn't have to admit it; it was written plainly on his face—a touching combination of protectiveness and unabashed desire. Richard had never seen him look that way before when talking about a girl.

It had been a very long time since Richard had felt that way, but he remembered it well enough to recognize it when he saw it. Michael was falling in love.

And, Richard was certain, Michael and Casey had made love.

What was it about the Cantrell women that held such a fatal fascination for the Bredon men? What caused such an intense physical attraction that demanded to be satisfied?

Unwillingly, Richard's thoughts were drawn back to the first time he and Jesse had made love. They hadn't known each other any longer, really, than Michael and Casey had. Was it only the third time they'd met? Yes, for it was right after that terrible night when the bombs fell . . . when he'd thought he'd lost her just as she'd come into his life so unexpectedly . . . before he'd even made her his. . . .

Jesse stopped and stared at the jeep, then at Richard sitting in the driver's seat. Cocking her head, she flashed the smile that sent a lusty roar through audiences night after night. "Who'd you steal it from? Is Eisenhower on foot at the moment?"

Richard grinned disarmingly. "A chap in the motor pool owed me a favor."

"Must've been a big one."

"It was. Hop in."

Jesse remained standing on the sidewalk just outside her flat. She looked almost heartbreakingly lovely in a dove-gray dress and matching hat with a wispy net veil. The hesitation she felt was obvious in the tense way she held herself. "I have a performance tonight."

"I know. But not this afternoon."

"Do you fly tonight?"

He met her look. "Yes."

The moment he answered, she knew the decision was made for her. She had absolutely no desire to walk away from him. Climbing into the jeep, she asked, "Where are we going?"

"The country."

As he drove off she held her hat firmly on her head and said, "I realize England isn't large, but even so you might be a little more specific."

He flashed her a sidelong glance. "It's a little place I know in Kent. I think you'll like it. It's quite charming."

She looked away. Whether the little place in Kent was charming or not didn't really matter, she knew. Sight-seeing wasn't on her mind . . . or Richard's.

They drove for an hour through the green English countryside. When it began to rain, Richard stopped and put the top on the jeep.

"Does it ever stop raining here?" Jesse asked, suddenly irritable.

Richard smiled ruefully. "Occasionally." Then, giving her a long, slow look, he added in a voice that had slipped into a lower register, "Don't worry. It'll be all right."

Her eyes met his in tacit understanding. Somehow she was no longer irritable.

Finally they stopped at an ancient inn made of stone; a faded sign that read "The Bear and Bull" creaked softly in the light wind. Inside, they sat at a wooden trestle table near a huge stone fireplace with a roaring fire. Richard drank tea and Jesse drank coffee and neither said very much.

"All the talk is of an invasion of France. Do you have any idea when it might come?" she asked.

He shook his head. "No. Only the top brass will know. They won't pass the information down till the last minute."

They both lapsed into silence again for several minutes.

Then, looking down at her cup, Jesse whispered, "I don't think I want any more coffee."

Richard's look was gentle, but tinged with expectancy. "I don't want any more tea, either."

Five minutes later they were in the only bedroom the inn offered to let.

Jesse felt like a virgin again. She and Frank had lived together for only one brief week before he'd shipped out. That was a year earlier. Since she'd come to England they'd shared only an occasional few hours' leave—until he'd gone on a top-secret mission to France a month earlier and never returned.

She figured out once that all in all they'd spent ten nights together in a year of marriage. Hardly enough to feel comfortable sexually, let alone to fully explore her sexuality.

Now, as she looked at Richard standing before her next to an old four-poster bed, she could read the hunger and need etched in his handsome face. She felt those things as well. But the force of their urgency left her breathless and uncertain.

"I don't know what to do," she admitted helplessly.

His slate-blue eyes softened with compassion. "Just let me hold you for a moment."

She stepped into his arms and leaned her cheek against his chest as he pressed her tightly against him.

He murmured against her hair, "All the way here, while you were sitting next to me, I wanted to touch you. To make sure you were real and not a dream. It was all I could do to keep my hands on the wheel."

"I'm real, Richard. I'm no dream, but a flesh-and-blood woman. And I want you so."

"Oh, God, Jesse, I want you, too."

"Tell me what to do."

"Just let me love you, sweetheart."

Then his lips were on hers, hot and seeking. An answering response welled up from deep within her. Need met need and ignited, exploded, became something greater. Somehow their clothes were off and they were in the goosedown bed under layers of blankets and a patchwork quilt. Jesse's awkwardness gave way to instinctive movements, and Richard responded as a drowning man would to a lifeline.

The urgency was too great to allow for a slow, careful exploration of each other. Each needed the release from constant tension that only the other could give. Jesse's nails dug into his back, Richard's teeth nipped her shoulder. She cried out once, then was silent. He groaned as if he were in pain—the agony of ecstasy.

It was a celebration of life, a defiance of the death that lay in wait day after endless day. When their passion exploded and they shuddered against each other, in that moment they felt a sense of triumph.

Afterward, they lay in each other's arms and said things they'd never said to another.

"When they told me Frank was missing and presumed dead, my first thought was disbelief. They didn't know him as I did. They didn't know how much he loved life and how hard he would fight to live. It was days before I accepted that he was gone, that he wouldn't come waltzing back into my life with his crooked smile and reckless charm."

Richard kissed her forehead and whispered, "Until I met you, I wasn't sure I wanted to live. When Roger died, I thought that was the worst that could happen. It terrified me to think of dying. Then, as I flew mission after mission, and saw the men I was responsible for—my friends—die, never knowing when it would be *my* turn, I realized there was something worse than death. What gets to you is not knowing when it will happen, if you'll go suddenly or die in agony."

He began to tremble slightly.

"Oh, Richard." Everything within Jesse yearned to comfort him. She drew his head onto her breasts and cradled it there, gently stroking his golden hair.

His trembling stilled. He went on, "After a while, you almost begin to hope for death. Just to get it over with."

Jesse murmured words of reassurance as Richard had done to her the night of the bombing.

After a while he raised his head and looked down at her. "Do you know what I thought when I first saw you?"

Her lips softened in a tender smile. "No."

"I thought you were lovely. I thought you had the most beautiful smile I'd ever seen. It lit up that whole theater. Just looking at you made me feel happy for the first time in years."

His words warmed her as no other words of praise or flattery ever had.

"Do you know what I thought of you when I first saw you?" she asked.

He shook his head.

"I thought you were the handsomest man I'd ever seen. Everything about you was so perfect."

He grimaced. "I'm not sure that's a compliment. Being perfect sounds rather unappealing, somehow."

"Oh, but you *were* appealing. Because deep in your beautiful blue eyes was a vulnerability that touched my heart. It was so obvious that you were afraid and were trying desperately to conceal it."

Richard smiled ruefully. "So much for stiff upper lips." The smile faded, and he went on soberly, "When I'm with you I'm not afraid."

"At this moment, I'm not afraid, either."

"Jesse, when I get my next leave I want to take you to Bredon Hall. I want you to see it."

"No, please, don't talk about it. Let's not make plans. Just . . . just be waiting there at Half-Moon Square when you can get leave."

He understood what she meant. It was more than just a superstitious refusal to count on something that might not happen. If she expected him and he didn't come . . . she would know the worst had happened. If she didn't expect him, she could tell herself he simply hadn't been able to get leave that day.

"All right," he agreed. Then a thought occurred to him, sending a troubled shadow over his face. "If I wait and *you* don't come, Jesse . . ."

"I'll be there."

"Promise?"

She smiled tenderly. "Cross my heart and hope to die."

They were silent for a long moment, lost in each other. Then Jesse realized the room had grown darker. It was getting late. She asked anxiously, "What time is it?"

Looking at his watch on the bedside table, Richard said, "It's only four o'clock. We have a little time left."

How little time? she wondered, thinking of the mission he must fly that night.

As if reading her thoughts, he assured her, "I'm going to be all right, Jesse. Now that I've found you, I'm not going to let anything happen. The ruddy Germans have had four years to shoot me down. They haven't managed to do it yet."

"Oh, Richard, I know it sounds silly, but promise me you won't die."

There wasn't a trace of humor in his expression as he responded, "I promise you, Jesse. I won't die."

She clung to him tightly. Though deep inside she knew it made no sense, she felt reassured by his promise.

Then, as her breasts brushed his chest and his legs were entwined with hers, both felt a restirring of passion. Gently he kissed her face—her eyelids, the tip of her nose, her chin. There was a tiny cleft in her chin.

"Where did you get that?" he teased in a husky voice.

"My mother told me when I was a little girl that it was God's thumbprint. She said it meant I was special."

His lips nuzzled her throat. "She was right."

"I thought it meant something special would happen to me. All my life I've waited for that. I finally decided I was being childish, and I stopped hoping. But now that I've met you . . ." She looked at him slowly. "I think my mother was right."

An hour later, the jeep pulled up in front of Jesse's flat. Jesse and Richard had both been silent on the drive back into London, the comfortable silence of two people who were at ease with each other, who didn't feel the need to make meaningless small talk just to pass the time.

Now, however, the silence was oppressive. Richard had no idea how to say good-bye, and Jesse didn't want to even hear the word.

"I'm due at the base in an hour. I'll barely make it," he said.

"I understand."

There was so much to say and no time to say any of it.

Jesse jumped down from the jeep. Then, as Richard put it into gear, she looked at him and said, "Remember your promise."

His voice was heavy with unexpressed emotion as he replied, "I'll remember."

He drove off.

Jesse watched until the jeep was engulfed in the traffic of London, then she turned and walked up the three flights of stairs to her flat. As she entered, she found Emily sitting in a chair, reading a book.

"Jesse, you're late. You've barely time to change for the theater."

"I know." Jesse walked into the tiny kitchen. As always, a pot of hot water sat warming on the stove. She made a cup of tea, then returned to the sitting room and sat down opposite Emily.

"Tea? I thought you hated the stuff."

"No time for coffee. And I . . . need something hot and soothing."

Emily put down her book and gave her a long, thoughtful look. "Something happened."

Jesse looked down, unable to meet her curious gaze.

"Jesse, we're friends, you know. I'd like you to think you can confide in me."

"I know we're friends, Emily. And it isn't that I'm trying to be secretive. I'm just not sure what's happened or how to talk about it."

Emily smiled warmly. "Why not begin at the beginning and go on until the end?"

"The beginning was two weeks ago in the Half-Moon Pub. And the end . . . well, I don't know what it will be, but I have an awful premonition it won't be happy."

At the mention of the Half-Moon Pub, Emily had gone still and her smile vanished. She said in a voice oddly unlike her own, "You've seen Richard again."

"Yes. Oh, Emily, I don't know what's happened. The world's been turned upside down for so long, I'm not sure if I can recognize it when it's right-side up. I only know that for a few hours today I was happy. I wasn't lonely, and I wasn't afraid."

Emily didn't respond immediately. She sat thinking quietly for a while. Then she said in a low voice, "I sensed something happening between you."

"Can you imagine it? Someone like Richard Bredon and *me*?"

"Since it's happened, of course I can imagine it."

The sudden coolness in Emily's tone reached Jesse, and an awful suspicion gripped her. "You told me you and Richard were old friends. Was there anything more? . . ."

"Don't be silly," Emily quickly replied. "As far as Richard's concerned, I'm the little sister he never had."

"And as far as you're concerned?"

Emily hesitated for just a fraction of a second, then responded with her old jovial manner, "He's my big brother, of course. I'm an only child. Growing up with Richard . . . well, I became very close to him."

Jesse still felt rather awkward somehow. "Then why do I get the feeling you don't approve of our relationship?"

"It's not a question of approving or disapproving. Jesse, you're a nice girl. And Richard's a nice chap, though a bit wild at times. It's just . . ."

Emily paused. It was clear she was trying to find a polite way to express what she was really feeling. Her eyes didn't quite meet Jesse's.

Jesse leaned forward in her seat waiting for Emily to continue.

Finally Emily met her look and began again. "It's hard for me to explain to you the kind of life Richard is used to. It's so different from what I imagined your life has been."

She stopped, and Jesse got the distinct impression she knew just what Emily was thinking. "You're trying to say we're not right for each other."

"Well, you come from different worlds. Oh, listen, let's not even discuss it any further. It's none of my business."

"No, I want to know what you think. Emily, you know Richard much better than I do. You know his family, the way of life he's used to. I've only spent a few hours with him, and I know so little about him."

"What can I tell you about him that would be of any use?"

"He asked me to visit Bredon Hall."

"Oh."

"You sound as if that wouldn't be a good idea."

"I don't mean to give that impression at all. It's entirely up to you."

"Would his mother be friendly, do you think?"

"She would be perfectly polite."

"That's not the same thing, as I think you know."

"Jesse, I don't know what to say. You want me to reassure you there would be no problems if you and Richard were seriously involved. But I can't give you that reassurance. There *would* be problems. I think you must know that, or you wouldn't even be talking to me this way."

Jesse admitted slowly, "Yes, I know there are problems."

Emily went on in a concerned tone, "You two have only just met. And with this damn war, sometimes people think they feel more than they do. It's that need to experience as much as possible, for tomorrow . . . well, there mayn't be a tomorrow."

Jesse didn't reply. Of course Emily would look on it that way. Just another wartime romance that would probably be over almost as soon as it had begun. Wasn't that more or less what she'd said to Richard the night of the bombing? And in her heart of hearts, wasn't that what she was afraid of now? That she was merely someone who gave him comfort at a time when he needed it badly, but not someone he could truly care for?

Her own feelings were far less of a mystery. She'd fallen in love with him today.

She set down her teacup. "I'd better change and get over to the theater."

Emily didn't say anything further. She didn't have to. She'd made her feelings quite clear.

Chapter Nine

The knock on the door surprised Casey. It was only five o'clock. Michael wasn't due for two hours. But when she opened the door, she found him standing there.

"You're a bit early," she said with a grin. Gesturing at her jeans and sweater, she added, "Obviously, I'm not exactly ready to go out."

Putting his hands on her shoulders, he kissed her forehead. "You look marvelous. But then, you'd look marvelous in a gunnysack."

"What an accomplished flatterer you are. You must've had lots of practice."

As he came into her room he responded, "Lots. But in your case it isn't flattery, it's the truth."

He sat down on the single chair, crossing one long leg over the other, as Casey sat down on the edge of the bed. Her smile faded and she said slowly, "Michael . . . I talked to a woman today who knew my mother."

He looked at her sharply. She didn't seem upset. Whatever the woman had told her, it must not have been what his father had told him.

Casey went on, "Her name is Rose Donovan and she knew your mother during the war."

"Rose Donovan? I don't recall my mother ever mentioning anyone by that name."

"Rose said she didn't see your mother after your parents' marriage. So it's been quite a while since they were friends. But the important thing is this: She told me my mother *was* here in London, during the war, and she knew your father."

"I know, Casey. I talked to my father this afternoon. He admitted knowing your mother during the war."

"He did? Then why did he lie to me?"

"I'm not sure." It was only partly a lie.

Casey's anger rose. "He accused me of attempting blackmail. And all the while, he knew—"

Michael interrupted, "He honestly wasn't sure of your motives in contacting him."

She glared at him. "That's a backhanded compliment if ever I heard one."

"Sorry. But it's the truth. Needless to say, I assured him he was wrong."

"Thanks."

Michael leaned toward her and took her hands in his. "I think you're confusing the message with the messenger."

His touch, the warm look in his eyes, melted her anger. "Oh, Michael, I'm sorry. I'm being . . ."

"Beastly?" he supplied.

She grinned. "Yes. Beastly. And none of it's your fault. It's just so frustrating. Nobody seems to want to help me get at the truth. Both your father and

Rose Donovan know more than they're willing to tell me."

Michael asked with studied casualness, "What did Rose Donovan say?"

Casey sighed. "Pretty much what your father said. My mother and your father knew each other. They were 'involved' somehow. But she wouldn't say *how* involved they were, or what happened to end the relationship."

Remembering what his father had said—"She was no good. Period."—Michael glanced away, unable to meet Casey's mystified look. He couldn't repeat those words to her. He'd never heard his father refer to any woman that way. The fact that he did so toward Jesse Cantrell could only mean the worst. The woman must have been pretty bad.

Whether she was or not, it would hurt Casey too much to go into it. He understood the need to think well of one's parents. If they're not all they should be, it's a hard truth to face. He knew that from firsthand experience with his own mother.

Casey was too caught up in remembering her unsatisfying meeting with Rose to notice that Michael was being very quiet. She went on unhappily, "It confirms what I was afraid of, though. When my mother knew your father, she was married."

"Casey, they wouldn't be the first couple to break marriage vows. Especially in wartime."

"But that just makes it even worse. My father was fighting, risking his life. He ended up being badly wounded. How could my mother do that to him?"

"Do you realize you're jumping to all sorts of dramatic conclusions? You could be all wrong about this. Perhaps my mother and your father were just friends."

"Is that what your father said?" she asked eagerly.

"No, not exactly. As I said, he really wouldn't say very much. Just that he knew her."

Casey was thoughtful for a moment. When she spoke, there was a note of poignancy in her tone that caught at Michael's heart. "I always thought my mother was perfect. Well, as perfect as anyone can be. She was so nice, everyone liked her. She never said or did a mean or spiteful thing in her life. I wanted to be like her, and when I realized I couldn't because I had quite a temper, I felt like a failure somehow."

"Casey . . ."

"I know what you're going to say. No one's that perfect."

He flashed that killer grin that sent a rush of feeling deep in her abdomen. "Actually, I was going to say I rather like your temper. I find it challenging."

"Do you really?"

"Yes. *Really*."

There was a pause. Does he mean it? Casey wondered.

Then Michael went on slowly, "My father said something I tend to agree with, though."

She shot him a defensive look. "What?"

"That he knew your mother forty years ago. *Forty years*, Casey. That was a long time ago, before either of us was even born. Whatever was between them ended then."

"But don't you see, Michael, it didn't end!"

"What do you mean?"

"The *letter*. My mother wrote that letter to him, even though she hadn't seen him in years. Whatever's in it, it's something that she felt was very important. There was *something* unresolved about their relationship."

"Casey, you're just guessing."

"I think it's a pretty good guess. Do you have a better explanation?"

Michael fumbled for some response. "Perhaps she simply wanted to let him know that she'd never forgotten him, or words to that effect. Something saccharine like that."

Casey's look was withering. "You didn't know my mother. She wasn't saccharine. She was kind of quiet, actually, and when she said something, she meant it. She wouldn't have gone to the trouble of writing that letter, then putting it aside for years and arranging for it to be delivered after her death, just to say 'I never forgot you.'"

Michael said compassionately, "I understand what you're saying, sweetheart. But the point is, it *was* a very long time ago. My father, and Rose Donovan, too, apparently, are suggesting that you let the past rest. It might very well be best for everyone concerned, including you." He looked at her. "*Especially* you."

She sighed and, letting go of his hands, lay back on the bed. Then, talking more to herself than to Michael, she said softly, "I don't know how to make you understand the depth of my feelings about this. I'm not at all sure I understand it myself. At first, when I found the letter, I thought it was a little odd. But I told myself it wasn't that big of a deal. Two weeks' vacation in London, during which I could deliver the letter, kill two birds, so to speak; then I'd return home and get on with my life."

She paused, trying to find just the right words to express how she felt. When she continued, she went slowly, thinking out each phrase before she spoke. "Then I got here and met your father. And suddenly it wasn't so simple anymore. Everything that I'd taken for granted—my parents' happy marriage, my mother's basic character—was suddenly brought into question. I didn't know what was true, what to believe. And what was even more disturbing was the fact that I began to sense there was some sort of mystery involved."

She stopped, frustrated. "No, mystery's not quite the right word. There's *something* here that needs to be straightened out. I don't know what it is exactly, but I have the strong feeling that it matters very much. That it shouldn't just be dropped." She looked at him with a wry smile. "Some vacation."

Michael got out of the chair and sat down on the bed beside Casey. He brushed her hair back from her face, then left his hand resting against the curve of her cheek. "Casey, my father doesn't want to delve into the past. Rose Donovan doesn't think it's a good idea. Can't you listen to them and forget all this?"

She shook her head. Her voice was small and confused but determined. "No, I can't forget it. Because I'm beginning to realize this has to do with me, too."

"How?"

"To a certain extent, I'm an extension of my mother. Certain things shaped her, made her what she was, and she, in turn, shaped me, made me what I am. I thought I knew her. Suddenly, I've discovered that I didn't. I can't understand myself until I understand her. Does that make sense to you?"

"Yes, but . . ."

"*But*. There are no *buts,* Michael. All my life I've had the vague feeling that something was wrong. Maybe not wrong, exactly, but *missing*. Some piece to the puzzle of my life. I'm beginning to think that it has to do with that letter. Or at least it has to do with whatever my mother wanted to communicate in that letter."

He couldn't argue with her further. As he'd already discovered, Casey was the kind of person who wanted the truth, not fantasy. No matter how hard it might be, she could face it. He wanted her to stop her search for the truth because he was afraid that what she would learn would ruin her memory of her mother. But he was beginning to realize that he couldn't stop her when she was this determined. All he could do was be there to offer comfort when she learned the worst.

It was a new feeling for him, this willingness to let someone else depend on him emotionally. It felt surprisingly nice, considering how long he'd resisted that kind of responsibility.

He looked down at Casey. What was it his father had said? "You've only just met." True. It had only been three days. Yet those three days seemed to hold more meaning than all the rest of his life.

His father had also said, "You don't know each other." That was true, too, in a way. He didn't know if Casey squeezed the tube of toothpaste in the middle or rolled it up from the bottom. She didn't know what his political beliefs were.

What he did know, and he knew it without a doubt, was that he needed her. And she needed him. Nothing else was as important as that. They would have the rest of their lives to learn the details about each other. In this short space of time, they'd already discovered the only thing that really mattered.

Whatever happened with her mother's letter, he wouldn't let their relationship be affected.

He smiled down at her. "Tell you what. Let's go out on the town. Dinner at some dark, romantic restaurant, a ride through Hyde Park in a hansom cab, then a nightcap at a quiet little place I happen to know of. It's very exclusive. We'll be the only two people there."

Casey's golden eyes were warm with anticipation. "Mm, sounds wonderful. Especially the part about the nightcap."

Bending down, he kissed the tip of her nose. "Have I told you yet that your freckles drive me insane with lust?"

She giggled. "No, you haven't. I seem to remember you commenting on other areas of my anatomy last night, but not my freckles."

"It's true. They're my secret passion. There's something about them—they're so innocent and childlike, and yet the rest of your delicious body is anything but innocent. And if you don't hurry up and dress, they'll send me into such a frenzy that I shan't be able to resist taking you here and now."

"*Before* dinner?"

"Yes. I realize it's something no well-bred Englishman should even admit, but there it is. Those lovely little golden spots drive all sense of propriety from my mind."

Casey put her arms around his neck and drew his lips down to hers. Just before they met, she whispered, "I've always thought propriety a highly overrated quality."

"What a coincidence. So have I—"

His words were cut off as their lips met. The long, breathless kiss made Casey's heart flutter. The feel of his hard chest pressing against her breasts produced a low, throbbing ache deep within her. What was it about this man that affected her so?

But there was no time to ponder the question. His hands had begun to draw slow, steady circles on her shoulders. It wasn't an overpoweringly erotic gesture, since there was a sweater between her skin and his fingertips. Yet it was a seductive invitation that beckoned irresistibly. She couldn't think any longer, she could only feel and act.

Gazing up at Michael through half-closed eyes, she whispered, "Undress me."

He didn't hesitate. With quick, deft movements, he removed her sweater and jeans. Then, looking at her plain white bra and panties, he said, "I'm going to buy you some incredibly sexy lingerie. Then thoroughly enjoy taking it off you."

As he unhooked the front snap of her bra, he bent down and buried his face in her breasts. He hadn't shaved since early that morning and his skin was slightly rough. Casey closed her eyes and luxuriated in the incredibly erotic sensation of that rough skin against the tender flesh of her breasts. When Michael lifted his head after a moment, she felt a sense of abandonment.

Hooking his thumbs in her bikini panties, he drew them down and tossed them on the floor where her other clothes lay in a jumble. Now she lay naked before him. The burning light in his eyes as he took in every curve and hollow of her body elicited a similar response within her.

"Now it's my turn," she whispered.

She slipped his tan gabardine jacket off his broad shoulders, then began unbuttoning his pale blue shirt. As each button came apart, revealing a tantalizing expanse of chest, Casey kissed the bare skin. Michael sighed blissfully and murmured her name as she continued until the last button was undone.

As she pulled the shirt down she rained featherlight kisses across his shoulders. At the same time, the tips of her breasts brushed against his chest, arousing them both even further. Casey had never before allowed herself to be so blatantly seductive, but with Michael she felt completely free.

Michael stood up beside the bed to make it easy for Casey to undo the snap at the waistband of his tan gabardine slacks. Slowly, enjoying every moment of the erotic suspense, she pulled down the zipper and watched as a ruddy triangle of golden-brown hair was revealed.

"Mm, a natural blond, I see," she quipped.

He threw back his head and laughed lustily. As his slacks fell to the floor, he encircled her in his arms, then pulled her down onto the bed. "A woman I can laugh with in bed—what more could I want?"

She returned his smile. It was entirely new, this sensation of having fun while making love, and it added a whole new aspect to sexuality.

"Michael Bredon, you tickle my fancy."

"Casey Cantrell, before I'm through, I intend to tickle a great deal more than just your fancy."

"Do you, now?"

"I do indeed."

"Well, be careful. I'm *very* ticklish."

His voice was husky. "So I've noticed."

Then he kissed her, blotting out everything else. Casey clung to him as their mouths sought each other greedily, tongues entwining, teeth sharply teasing beneath the soft fullness of their lips. Michael straddled her with his legs as his hands kneaded her shoulders.

As she was pinned beneath him he rose up on his knees to look down at her. The iron strength in those lean legs amazed and aroused her. Then she remembered Michael was an experienced rider: it took a great deal of strength and ability to control a fifteen-hundred-pound horse.

The sprinkling of coarse hair on his legs rasped teasingly against the smoothness of her thighs. As he looked down at her the light in his eyes was no longer humorous, but fierce. She sensed a profound need in him that went deeper than physical desire. Casey wasn't at all sure what prompted it; she only knew that she wanted to meet it, wanted to fill the emptiness revealed in the lost look that lay behind his usual mocking expression.

His fingertips had moved from her shoulders to her breasts, where they stroked and caressed with an incredibly light touch.

Casey's breath came hard and fast now as she felt her nipples grow taut beneath Michael's gently circling thumbs. Each movement of his hands sent shivers of violent pleasure through her. Then he bent down to take each tip in his mouth, first flicking his tongue across the nipple, then teasing her with his teeth. Casey arched her back and writhed beneath him.

"Michael. Oh, Michael, make love to me."

"I will, darling. But first you'll make love to me."

"What?"

Dazed by her growing need, she didn't understand at first. But when he wrapped his arms around her and rolled over so that she was on top of him, she understood. The idea of playing a new role excited her. Placing her hands on his shoulders, she rose and positioned herself over him. He was more than ready for her, and in an instant he'd penetrated her. After the first shock of feeling him inside her, she began to move slowly against him, raising and lowering her body in a slowly building rhythm.

Her hair fell past her face, and as she bent to kiss him it enveloped both of them. When she lifted her head he ran his fingers through her hair, glorying in its silken feel and inhaling its sweet scent. Then his hands moved to her hips in a firm but gentle grip. His touch urged her on and she began moving faster.

Her rapid movement and his powerful response produced a contact that was electric. Heat met heat, force met moist smoothness. Casey's fingers dug into his shoulders, but if it hurt him, he didn't seem to care. His hands cupped her round, soft derriere now, moving with her rhythmic motion.

Michael's face was flushed, his golden skin damp with perspiration. As Casey's breasts moved up and down before him, he raised up his head and flicked the nipples with his tongue. The quick, whiplike movement sent shiver after shiver coursing through her each time she felt his moist tongue.

Casey's eyes were closed, her breathing erratic, as she went on and on. She felt as if she were on a roller coaster, heading slowly but inevitably toward the top of the steepest downturn. Any moment now, she knew, she would reach the top, and then it would be a long, terrifyingly ecstatic race down.

Just as she felt herself reaching that peak, Michael's hands went to her shoulders, then his arms encircled her and he rolled her over beneath him, remaining inside her.

"Now," he whispered in a voice hoarse with need.

At that moment, he thrust deep within her, panting and lunging. All awareness left him save the scent and feel of this woman. The force of his rapture swept Casey up to the peak and she began a descent past all reason and control, into an ecstasy of sensation. She buried her face against his chest to muffle the cries that were torn from deep within her.

For several minutes they lay together, Michael still and spent, Casey quivering with a joy that seemed to know no end. Then he slipped off her and they got under the bedclothes. He pulled her against him tightly, as if unwilling to let her be even a hairs-breadth away from him. She cradled her head against his shoulder and felt like a child in his arms. His breath gently ruffled the hair at her temple.

Neither spoke. Words were unnecessary . . . and inadequate, anyway. Casey didn't have to ask if Michael had felt what she had felt. It was achingly apparent in his face, transformed by gentleness now, and his body, lying against hers as if it had always done so.

I love him, she thought sleepily. There was no surprise in the revelation.

It was ten o'clock that night before they awoke, dressed and went to dinner. Neither felt like going to a restaurant. Each wanted to continue being just with the other. So they went to Michael's flat and Casey made cheese omelets while Michael toasted sourdough muffins. They took the food, and a bottle of white wine, into the living room. There they sat on the floor in front of the fire that Michael had started in the fireplace and ate and drank.

Casey's appetite was enormous. She felt as if she were half-starved, as if this were the best meal she'd ever tasted.

Michael's eyes and lips were warm with a smile as he watched her. "I can see I'll go bankrupt feeding you."

She returned his smile. "My mother used to tease me about my appetite."

He looked at her soberly. "In case you weren't aware of it, that was a subtle way of asking you to marry me."

She stopped, stunned. She hadn't expected this, not yet. Perhaps never.

He went on, "I apologize if it wasn't a very romantic proposal. But I haven't had much practice. You're the first one I've asked."

Casey put down her fork and pushed her plate away. Then she took a long sip of wine. Her head was spinning—and not from half a glass of wine.

Finally she met Michael's look. "It was a wonderful proposal."

"But?"

"But . . . we've only just met and we don't know very much about each other—"

He stopped her torrent of awkward words with a fingertip placed gently against her lips. "Ssh. You're speaking nonsense, and you know it. What's between us is so right it doesn't require time or thought."

"But Michael, this is crazy."

"Yes. Crazy and wonderful."

"Are you *sure*?"

He nodded.

"But how can you be?"

"Casey, I spent a long time looking for love, waiting to feel what other people seemed to feel so easily. Finally, I gave up. I decided it was either an illusion or . . . or I just didn't have what it took to feel that way about anyone. So I had brief affairs, and occasionally longer relationships, sometimes with women I genuinely liked and respected. But I was never in love. *Never.* Until now."

"Is that why you never married?"

"Yes. I considered it once or twice. Out of loneliness, basically. But I knew it would be unfair to the woman I would marry. And I didn't want to have the kind of marriage my parents have, an empty shell for convention's sake. I wanted emotion, commitment, fire."

He looked at her and added, "All the things I feel with you right now."

"Right now. What about later? This could just be a physical attraction . . . infatuation."

Michael chuckled softly. "Sweetheart, I'm no impressionable kid. I'm thirty-eight years old. I'll be thirty-nine in three months. I've had infatuations. I'm no saint, Casey. Which isn't particularly admirable, except I can honestly say I've experienced enough to know my own feelings. What I feel for you is something I've never felt before—and am not likely to ever feel with anyone else."

Her golden-brown eyes were troubled. "I've been accused of being rash and impulsive. But at this moment I feel like I want to be very, very careful."

"It's too late to be careful, sweetheart. The die is cast."

Suddenly she felt terribly nervous and unsure. "Let's be practical about this, Michael."

He burst into laughter. "Practical?" He put his arms around her and leaned her back against the sofa. "All right, we'll be practical. Instead of rushing up to Scotland, where marriage is a quick, easy affair, we'll have a formal ceremony here. Or in Kentucky. Wherever you wish."

"Michael, we don't know each other."

"You said that."

"But you didn't hear me."

He sighed. "All right, then, let's get to know each other. Move in with me. But I warn you, even if I discover that you snore, I intend to marry you."

She couldn't help smiling. His sense of humor was one of his more potent attractions.

As if reading her thoughts, he said huskily, "We laugh together, we excite each other. What else is there to be concerned about?"

"A million things. What if we disagree violently about politics?"

"I'm not a violent person when it comes to political beliefs. In fact, I'm boringly middle of the road. And you?"

She was the same. Ignoring that, she went on, "Children, for instance; we haven't even discussed whether or not we would want children."

"All right. Do you want children?"

She looked into those turquoise eyes and was lost. "I want *your* children."

He was profoundly touched. "And I would most definitely want yours, Casey. The thought of you carrying my child is the loveliest thing imaginable."

She searched for other areas of possible disagreement. "I'm pretty old-fashioned, Michael, when it comes to marriage."

"You mean in terms of fidelity?"

She nodded.

"Well, darling, there's no one more straitlaced than a reformed philanderer. And I am thoroughly reformed."

"You seem able to counter all my arguments."

"That's because they don't matter a damn. The only thing that matters is that I've found you when I had given up hope of ever having such happiness within my grasp."

She was silent, unable to think of anything further to say.

Watching her, he said in a more concerned voice, "Are you worried about having to move here? I can see where that would seem rather a formidable thing to do."

Actually she hadn't even thought about whether or not she would miss Kentucky. Her mind had been entirely focused on being with Michael. She was mildly surprised to realize that she wouldn't care where she lived as long as he was there. What was the old saying? "Home is where the heart is." Her heart was with this man . . . now and forever.

Clearly worried that he'd brought up a sensitive subject, Michael hastened to assure her, "You wouldn't have to leave Kentucky permanently. In fact, perhaps we could live in both places. I've been wanting to go over there to check out the stock. It's generally accepted that Kentucky has the best stallions. With those stallions and Bredon mares, who knows what we might accomplish?"

Casey smiled up at him. "I suspect that even Hamdan, with all his money, couldn't accomplish as much."

A look of relief crossed Michael's face. "Then if that's all right, there are no problems, Casey."

"You're forgetting one major problem."

"What?"

"Your father."

The two brief words hung in the air between them, an invisible barrier. Finally Michael responded slowly, "He'll come around, Casey. You've seen him at his worst, but believe me, he's normally a kind and reasonable man. It will be all right."

She shook her head. "No. It won't be all right as long as my mother's letter hangs over us."

"Casey, that has nothing to do with us."

"But it does. It's a shadow from the past, falling over the present."

"*Now* is all that matters, Casey. This moment."

"I wish that were true, Michael. But it isn't. The past colors everything. How can we start a new life together when there's something important unresolved from our old life?"

There was an undeniable truth to her words and Michael was silent for several minutes. Finally he said slowly, "What are you saying, then?"

"That I have to resolve this thing with my mother and your father before I can think about you and me."

Everything about her—the stubborn tilt of her chin, the tense way she held herself—showed that she wasn't about to be dissuaded.

"All right," he agreed heavily. "But I want you to move in with me tonight."

"Michael . . ."

"No arguments, Casey. I don't agree with your need to dig up the past, but I accept it. However, I don't want you out of my sight until this thing's resolved and I know there's no chance of losing you."

She looked at him tenderly. "There's no chance of losing me."

The moment was electric. Their eyes met in silent acknowledgment of mutual need. He cupped her face in his hands and kissed her gently. But even as she lost herself in him once more, she wasn't sure she'd spoken the truth.

Chapter Ten

The next morning Casey checked out of the Viscount Hotel. Michael had given her a key to his flat and told her he would be home as early as possible. After taking her luggage to the flat, she called Rose.

"Casey, I'm so glad to hear from you. I tried to reach you at your hotel and they said you'd checked out."

"Yes, I'm staying with . . . a friend."

"I meant to tell you yesterday that you're more than welcome to stay here. Are you sure you're quite comfortable where you are?"

Casey suppressed a smile. "Yes, quite. But thanks for the offer."

"It's open-ended. Any time you wish, just move right in. I have three empty bedrooms, and I'd adore the company."

"Rose, could I see you again this morning?"

"Of course. Come right over. And plan to stay for lunch. I'll make something special."

"Thank you. Bye."

When Casey arrived at Rose's house a few minutes later, she was greeted with a big hug as before.

"My, but you look lovely today. London agrees with you."

Casey felt a slight flush creep over her cheeks. Before she could think of a suitable response, Rose led her into the kitchen and motioned to a chair by a table. "Sit down and we'll have a nice chat while I shell peas. By the way, do you like peas and lamb chops?"

"Love them."

"Oh, good. That's what I've planned for lunch. And I got a sinfully delicious chocolate torte from an Austrian bakery down the street."

"Rose, you're being so kind."

"It's not kindness at all. As I told you, I thought a great deal of your mother. Over the years, I've wondered how you were. I'm very glad for the opportunity to know you now."

Casey sensed there was an underlying meaning to the apparently innocent remark. But as she looked at Rose, sitting placidly at the other end of the small butcher-block table, she decided she was imagining things. This business of her mother's relationship with Richard Bredon had her looking for hidden meanings everywhere.

"Rose, tell me about my mother. When you knew her, that is. What was she like?"

"I have a picture of the two of us together. Would you like to see it?"

"Oh, yes."

Rose went to a cupboard and took out a thick photo album, then returned to the table and laid it down. "I searched all evening looking for this.

Finally found it under my husband's old uniform in a trunk."

Turning the pages, she muttered, "Let's see, where is that picture?"

Casey caught glimpses of faded old black-and-white photographs—men in uniform, women with pompadour hairstyles and knee-length flowered dresses.

Suddenly Rose stopped. "This is it. Your mother and I. It was taken in the winter of 1944, just before . . ." Rose stopped, then went on quickly, "Just before she returned to the States."

Casey had seen other photos of her mother when she was young, but none from that time period. She looked at it carefully. Her mother wore a close-fitting dress of some muted color. Her hair was pulled back in a bun at the nape of her neck, and on her head was a smart little hat with a net veil. She looked more sophisticated than she had later in her life—and very beautiful.

"I was with her when she bought that outfit," Rose reminisced. "Cost five dollars, a lot of money in those days. She called it her 'going home' dress. Said she was going to wear it when the war was over and she and your father went back to the States."

"Rose . . . did she love my father?"

Rose gave her a warm look of understanding. "Yes, she did. She was absolutely loyal to him, Casey, if that's what you're wondering. I've never known a woman who was more loyal to a man."

"You said that she wasn't able to see much of my father. And, as someone else pointed out to me, it *was* wartime. I suppose it would be natural if she . . . well, if she was involved with other men. And she was very pretty."

"Casey, listen to me. It's true it was wartime and there were pressures . . . well, pressures that you can't begin to understand now. Many people took what comfort they could wherever they could find it. I didn't judge them. I understood and felt sorry for them."

"Was my mother one of those people?"

"No." At Casey's look of disbelief, Rose insisted, "I'm telling the truth, Casey. Your mother would never have done anything to hurt your father. That was one of the reasons I admired her so. As you said, she was extremely pretty. And singing in the theater night after night, she met a great many soldiers. But she behaved like a lady."

"Are you telling the truth, Rose? Or simply trying to spare my feelings?"

"I'm telling you the truth. Whatever is going through your mind about your mother, you can rest assured of one thing. She behaved with honor. And she showed more courage than most people are ever called upon to show."

"Then what about Richard Bredon?"

Rose sighed heavily. "You won't forget about that, will you?"

"I can't. Not until I've done as my mother wished and delivered that letter to him. Or at least unraveled the mystery of their relationship."

Rose shook her head. "Casey, Casey. What am I to do with you?"

"You could tell me the whole truth about my mother's relationship with Lord Bredon."

Rose responded guardedly, "I told you—they knew each other. Isn't that enough?"

"Why did he give her the pendant?"

"What pendant?"

"This one." Casey took it out of her purse and handed it to Rose. For a moment Rose simply held it, looking at it as if it were a relic from a time long past. As, in a sense, it was.

"This meant a great deal to your mother," she whispered.

"Why?"

"Oh, because it meant a great deal to Lord Bredon, I suppose."

"Why did he give it to her?" Casey pressed.

"I'm really not sure. Honestly."

Casey was silent for a moment. Rose went back to shelling peas, clearly reluctant to answer any more questions about Jesse and Richard Bredon. And Casey felt rude for pressing her. More than rude, thoughtless: for in asking about that time she was reminding Rose of her husband, who had died young.

She decided to approach the subject from a less sensitive standpoint. "What was it like then, Rose? During the war, I mean."

Rose leaned back in her chair and was thoughtful for a moment. "Well, it's hard to make you understand. You've never gone through anything like it. The entire world was at war, you see. The lines were clearly drawn—good versus evil. Tremendous sacrifices were required of everyone and were made gladly. Also, we didn't know how it would end. The enemy was powerful, and for a long time—until 1944, really—we weren't at all sure we would win."

She stopped and smiled. "But it wasn't all grim. There was a camaraderie, a sense of all being in it together. I suppose the overriding thing was that the best was demanded of all of us. And, for the most part, we gave our best. It meant a great deal then to feel we were doing the right thing."

"In a way, it was much simpler then."

"Yes, in a way. And we were so young, we had so much energy and zeal." She smiled wryly. "I know the young think the old can't remember what it was like when they were young. But we can. We had hopes and dreams and fears. And because we were young, we felt them with all our heart."

"What was my mother like when she was young?"

"She was full of life. She fairly sparkled. Lit up a room when she walked into it."

The description sounded nothing like the woman Casey had known, and she said so.

Rose responded soberly, "Well, we do change as we get older. Especially if we have an experience that forever alters our lives."

She looked at Casey, and for an instant Casey thought she would say something more. But she didn't.

Finally Casey admitted hesitantly, "I met Richard Bredon's son, Michael."

"Did you? What's he like now?"

"*Now?* Have you met him?"

Rose looked chagrined. When she spoke it was a bit too rapidly, as if she were trying to cover up a mistake. "Well, only once, years ago. He was just a boy. I ran into him somewhere."

"Oh, I see. Well, to answer your question, he's . . ." She stopped, unsure what to say. When she went on, her voice sounded false. "Well, he's very nice."

Rose cocked her head and eyed her curiously. "Casey, how many times have you seen Michael?"

"Several."

Casey looked down at her hands fiddling nervously in her lap. Then, aware of Rose's eyes boring into her, she forced herself to look up and ask, "May I help with those peas?"

Rose shook her head. "No, thank you. I'm nearly done. Casey, I don't mean to pry, but may I ask—is your interest in your mother's relationship with Richard Bredon affected by your relationship with Michael?"

"Yes. It is."

"Oh, my dear." Rose's voice was filled with concern.

"Is something wrong?"

"No, of course not." Then, as if it had just occurred to her, she added, "But you've only just arrived in London. When did you meet him?"

Briefly, leaving out some of the more personal details, Casey related her initial meeting with Michael and their subsequent meetings. "We've . . . gotten to know each other rather quickly," she finished, embarrassed.

Rose smiled gently. "So I see. I take it you don't have a young man back in Kentucky?"

"No."

"Michael was a compelling child. Not exactly beautiful, as some little boys are, but very appealing in an intense sort of way. I imagine he grew up to be quite an attractive man."

Casey admitted with some embarrassment, "He did indeed."

Suddenly a thought occurred to her. "Rose . . . you mentioned that you knew Michael's mother during the war. Was that at the same time you knew my mother?"

A guarded expression crossed Rose's face. "Yes."

"Did his mother know my mother?"

Rose hesitated, clearly unsure how to answer. Finally she said reluctantly, "Yes, they knew each other. But only for a short while. They weren't . . . especially close."

Setting aside the shelled peas, Rose stood up and moved to the sink. "I'd better get these on, or we shan't have any lunch. The lamb chops are already baking. Don't they smell delicious?"

Casey knew she was purposely changing the subject. Instead of forcing the conversation back to a topic Rose clearly didn't want to discuss, she replied, "They do."

Rose bustled about the kitchen, making the final preparations for lunch. She talked as she worked, keeping up a steady stream of light conversation.

The small, white-tiled kitchen was filled with the aroma of food cooking and with Rose's friendly, cheerful presence. Casey felt almost content—almost, but not quite. There were still so many unanswered questions.

As Rose put the peas on the stove, she said, "Tell me about your life in Kentucky. Do you still live on your parents' farm?"

"Yes." For a while Casey talked of the farm, of the horses she cared for and the young riders she taught.

Then lunch was ready. They ate in Rose's exquisite dining room, with its flowered wallpaper and French doors opening onto a small brick patio. There were no flowers in bloom on this cold autumn day, but tubs of shrubbery provided a backdrop of greenery.

Casey made a point of talking about general things—Rose's plans for her retirement, which had taken place a few months earlier, Rose's son and daughter-in-law who lived in Scotland and ran a country inn, and the pride and joy of Rose's life, her twin granddaughters, who visited her often.

"Ruth and Rachel both want to go to school here in London. Ruth fancies herself an actress and wants to attend RADA, the Royal Academy of Dramatic Arts. Rachel is the pragmatic one. She wants to attend the London School of Economics."

Casey smiled. "It's funny, isn't it, how two children from the same family, even children as close as twins, can be so different."

"Yes, it is. It just goes to show that we do make our lives what we want them to be, basically. Some people like to think it's all environment or all heredity. But I believe in the old maxim 'I am captain of my soul, I am master of my fate.'"

"Perhaps." Though Casey agreed with Rose to a certain extent, she also had the feeling one's past could affect the present and future, whether one wanted it to or not.

She said as much, and Rose replied thoughtfully, "I suppose that's true. There's a psychological theory—it's called the theory of social heritage, I believe. And it basically states that certain traits or types of behavior run in families. That's why you see people make the same mistake, generation after generation. A sixteen-year-old becomes an unwed mother, and later her daughter does the same. It's not accident or coincidence. It's a more deep-seated conditioning on the part of the members of that family."

Casey was struck by the force of Rose's words. Could it be, she wondered, that she was repeating her mother's life—perhaps her mother's mistake? Jesse had come to London and become involved with an English aristocrat. Now Casey was doing the same.

As she left later, Casey had a great deal on her mind.

Late that afternoon Casey sat in Michael's flat, looking out a huge round window at a fabulous view of London. She'd left her suitcases, still packed, sitting near the door. The more she'd thought about staying with Michael, the more uncomfortable she'd felt about it. She would accept Rose's invitation, she decided.

Then she heard a key in the door and a moment later Michael came in, carrying a grocery bag.

"Hi. I stopped and picked up some marvelous-looking lobster and a bottle of Montrachet. The lobster's alive and kicking. We'd better cook it quickly before it makes an escape. Tonight, *I'm* cooking. Just to allay any fears you may have that I might not be willing to do my fair share in the kitchen."

Placing the bag on a table, he bent down and took her face in his hands. He whispered, "I missed you today," and kissed her tenderly.

It was a sweet, gentle kiss, not designed to arouse her. Even so, she felt a vague stirring that she knew could be easily whipped into a raging inferno if Michael chose to do so. Would she always want him like this? she wondered.

The answer came swift and sure. Always.

"You're being very quiet," Michael went on, sitting down next to her on the sofa.

She leveled a direct look at him. Better to get it over with, she decided. "I saw Rose again today. Rose Donovan."

"Yes?"

"She offered to let me stay with her."

"But we agreed you're staying here."

She hesitated. As she did so, Michael's expression, which had been cheerful, grew sober. "Casey, you haven't changed your mind, have you?"

She nodded. Before he could argue, she spoke quickly. "Everything is moving too fast. I need time to think. I've never lived with a man before. I'm not even sure I think it's right."

"Is it more right to sleep here all night with me, then go elsewhere simply to shower and change?"

It was the brutal truth.

He could see she was wavering, acknowledging a conflict, but there remained that stubborn set to her chin Michael had already come to know so well.

He continued, "I don't think living together is a terribly good idea, either. It smacks of playing around rather than being serious. As I told you last night, I'd much rather marry you right this minute." He finished in a tone Casey had never heard him use before, "I love you, Casey. With all my heart."

"Oh, Michael, I love you, too." Suddenly she was sure of it. The doubts that had plagued her all day, especially since her conversation with Rose, disappeared as she looked into his turquoise eyes.

"Then let's get married right away. Later we'll have a formal reception. But for now I just want to make you mine without delay."

She shook her head. "I can't. Not yet." At his angry look she went on, "Please don't argue with me. Just try to understand."

He sighed heavily. "All right. I don't understand, but I won't argue with you. At least say you'll stay here with me."

"Michael, this isn't my home, it's yours. I feel like an interloper."

"I see. Well, *that* I can understand. Would you like to redecorate this place? Or find an entirely new flat?"

"I don't know."

"I honestly don't care where we live. As long as we're together."

Casey smiled at him. "You are too good to be true."

He returned her smile. "That's one thing I've never been accused of before."

"All right. I'll stay."

He put his arms around her and pulled her into a long, lingering kiss that was far less innocent this time. Within Casey, the banked embers that had been lightly stirred before now burst into flame. When Michael finally pulled away she asked in a breathless, teasing voice, "What about dinner?"

"Infuriating woman, all you think of is food."

"Not all." She put her arms around his neck and gave him a sly, seductive look.

He picked her up as easily as if she were a rag doll and headed toward his bedroom.

"What about the lobster?" she asked in mock concern.

"It can amuse itself. While we do the same."

For the next two weeks, Casey lived in a dream-world. Often she visited the farm with Michael, where they went on long, enjoyable rides. She looked over the horses with him and was gratified when he asked for her opinion on various problems that arose. Bredon Stud was a magnificent place, where Casey immediately felt at ease. The world of horses was one she knew and loved as well as Michael did. She seemed to fit right into that aspect of his life.

In fact, she fit right into the entire fabric of his life. They spent most evenings alone at home, because that was what both preferred. But occasionally Michael took Casey out, showing her London. She discovered they enjoyed doing many of the same things, from watching plays to trying new, unusual restaurants.

As time passed she was reassured to find that they got along as well out of bed as in. Her worry that their relationship was based on a physical infatuation lessened.

However, her concern over her mother's letter, and what to do about it, didn't lessen. Each day she took it out of her suitcase and looked at it, as if willing it to give up its secret.

Though she saw Rose occasionally, she hadn't been able to persuade her to give out any more information. Michael didn't mention his father, but Casey was sure Richard was still refusing to have anything to do with her.

There was one other person she could ask, though, someone she'd avoided approaching up to this point. But as time passed and she was unable to find any answers elsewhere, she decided she would have to see that person. So one morning when Michael was at the farm, Casey took a taxi to Belgravia, to his mother's house.

Belgravia was one of the most exclusive and fashionable residential areas of London. Monumental white stucco mansions, built in the early 1800s, were set off by pleasant little squares. Lady Emily Bredon's house was one of the smaller mansions but was nevertheless very imposing. As Casey lifted the brass lion's-head knocker on the black-enameled door, she felt even more nervous than when she'd approached Richard Bredon.

A young maid, blond and fair, wearing a crisp black-and-white uniform, answered promptly.

"Yes, miss?"

"I'd like to see Lady Bredon, please."

"I'll have to see if Her Ladyship's at home, miss. Whom shall I say is calling?"

"Casey Cantrell."

The maid left her standing just inside a wide black-and-white-tiled entryway as she disappeared into a room at the far end of the center hall. Casey stood there, clutching her purse, looking at the magnificent antiques that decorated the entryway—a black chinoiserie cabinet and matching mirror and a large jade figurine of an Oriental lady. She felt more than a little awkward and uncomfortable in the black pumps and heather-colored wool suit she'd bought recently when she'd realized she hadn't brought nearly enough clothes for what was turning out to be an extended stay in London.

Finally, after what seemed a very long time, the maid returned. "Her Ladyship will see you, miss. Right this way, please."

The girl led Casey into the room at the end of the hall. As Casey entered, the girl announced, "Miss Casey Cantrell, ma'am," and closed the door after her.

The peach-colored walls of the small sitting room were covered with old paintings and photographs.

The white French provincial furniture looked old and vaguely shabby, the way genuine antiques often look. Everything about the room reflected restrained good taste and inherited wealth.

The woman standing in the center of the room suited her surroundings. She was tall and slim, with erect posture. Her graying blond hair was swept back in a knot low on the nape of her neck. A single strand of pearls glistened on the bodice of her gray cashmere sweater. The matching pleated skirt hung modestly just below her knees.

Everything about her spelled "lady."

She would have been attractive, but there was a rigid set to her features. This wasn't someone who could be confided in, Casey decided immediately. She wondered how this woman could have produced a son like Michael, with his easy humor and fiery passion. It was hard to imagine this woman ever laughing—and impossible to imagine her in the throes of passion. No wonder her marriage was, as Michael had said, "an empty shell for convention's sake."

"Miss Cantrell?"

The voice was as cold as marble.

Casey crossed the room and extended her hand. "Lady Bredon."

The woman took the proffered hand, but only for a moment; then she let it drop. She didn't invite Casey to sit down.

"I'm afraid I haven't had the pleasure of your acquaintance, Miss Cantrell."

"No, but I believe you knew my mother, Jesse Cantrell, during the war."

There was the merest flicker of something—not

surprise—on Lady Bredon's face. So, Casey thought, she'd recognized the name when the maid gave it. Though it had been forty years, she hadn't forgotten Jesse, a woman Rose had insisted Lady Bredon hardly knew.

Lady Bredon said quietly, "It was some time ago when I last saw your mother. May I ask why you are approaching me now?"

"I saw Rose Donovan."

At the mention of Rose's name, Lady Bredon went white. She had been cool and composed, but now there was no mistaking the real fear that shone in her cold blue eyes. She sat down heavily on the satin brocade sofa.

Casey waited for a moment to be invited to sit also. When she wasn't, she simply sat down anyway. This was no time to stand on ceremony.

"What did Rose tell you?" Lady Bredon asked sharply.

"She told me that you and my mother were friends during the war."

"That was all?"

The question was clearly a crucial one. Lady Bredon sat tensely, waiting for Casey's answer.

"Yes, that was all."

"And your mother—did she ever speak of . . . of me?"

"No, she didn't. She didn't speak of the war at all. In fact, until I met Rose, I'd had no idea my mother was over here then."

Lady Bredon had too much control to breathe a sigh of relief. But Casey was sure that was exactly what she wanted to do.

Casey went on carefully, "I came over here for

personal reasons. I met your husband and your son."

"You know Michael?"

"Yes."

"Miss Cantrell, why have you come to see me?"

"I was hoping you could give me some information about my mother during the period when she was here."

"I'm afraid I didn't know your mother very well. We shared a flat, but only for a short time, perhaps two months. We each had our own work, our own lives. We weren't at all close."

"But you must've gotten to know her at least a little. If you lived together . . ."

"That was a very long time ago," Lady Bredon snapped.

It was a phrase Casey was getting used to hearing.

"Yes, I know that, but if you could just answer a few questions for me."

"I'm sorry, Miss Cantrell, but I can't do that. I remember almost nothing about your mother, beyond her name and the fact that we briefly shared a flat. Now if you'll excuse me . . ." She rose and finished in a firm tone, "I'm really very busy."

Casey stood up and hesitated for a moment. She wanted to press Lady Bredon further, but she suspected it would do no good at all. This wasn't a woman who could be pressured into anything.

"Thank you for seeing me," she finally replied politely.

Lady Bredon rang a bell and in a moment the maid returned. "Please show Miss Cantrell out, Leslie."

As Casey followed the girl outside, she felt thoroughly frustrated. And more than a little angry.

Michael was sitting in his office at Bredon Stud that afternoon when his mother pulled up outside. At the sight of her white Jaguar sedan through the window, he thought irritably, What the hell is she doing here?

His mother rarely came to Bredon Hall and never to the farm. It had been weeks since Michael had heard from her and months since he'd actually seen her. Now, as she walked in the door, he steeled himself to look more welcoming than he felt.

He rose as she walked in and crossed around his desk to dutifully kiss her cheek. "Mother. This is quite a surprise. What brings you all the way out here?"

She slipped off her tan suede driving gloves and laid them across her black patent-leather purse. As Michael leaned back against his desk, she sat down in a chair facing him.

"A young woman named Casey Cantrell came to see me today."

At the mention of Casey's name, Michael stiffened. He'd hoped that as time passed, Casey's need to unravel her mother's past would lessen. Obviously, he'd been wrong.

Emily went on coolly, "I don't like being approached by strange young women, Michael. She mentioned knowing you. Was she lying?"

"Of course she wasn't."

"You're . . . friends?"

He gave his mother a hard look. "You may as well know now that Casey and I are much more than friends. I've asked her to marry me."

"What!"

It was the first time in Michael's memory that he could recall his mother looking absolutely stunned. It was a relief, in a way, to discover that her iron control could actually slip.

"I was going to inform you when we'd actually decided on a date."

"That would have been very considerate of you," Emily said witheringly. "When did all this take place, may I ask?"

"Recently."

"It must have been very recent. How on earth did you meet her?"

"We ran into each other. She's visiting over here."

"What does your father think of this sudden notion of yours?"

"It isn't a *notion*, Mother. And it doesn't matter what he thinks. Or you, for that matter. Casey and I will be married as soon as possible."

"I must say, Michael, your manners haven't improved one bit since I last saw you. You've never had the proper respect for me, and considering your age, I despair of you ever developing it."

As Michael looked at her, the old hostility welled up within him. He and his mother had never been close. She wasn't openly rejecting; in fact, she was a dutiful mother in all the superficial ways. But Michael had always sensed that she didn't really love him. As a child he'd assumed it was his fault: he was somehow lacking. If only he tried harder, he would win her love. So he had worked hard at being perfect. But no matter how well he did in school, no matter how well behaved he was, no matter what carefully made gifts he labored over for her, she still made him feel he wasn't entirely accepted by her.

As a teenager he'd stopped trying to win her love and gone in the opposite direction—rebelling in every way imaginable. Only his close relationship with his father had kept him from becoming totally self-destructive. Now he faced the fact that he didn't want to have anything to do with this woman—and he certainly didn't want her interfering in his relationship with Casey.

"Let's be honest with each other. You've never particularly liked me and I don't like you."

"Michael!"

"It's time we were honest, at least. Since I've known Casey, I've realized the difference between merely being polite and genuinely caring about someone."

"Michael, you can't be serious about that girl."

"Why not?"

"She's not your kind."

His smile held no humor. "Somehow, I expected you to say that."

"Listen to me . . . *please*." There was a note of pleading in Emily's voice that took Michael by surprise. "I agree that we haven't been as close as we should have been, perhaps. But I have always done my best for you. I honestly have. You've had every advantage. You've certainly been better off than you would have been if . . ." She stopped, then went on, "Than you would have been if you'd been born into less fortunate circumstances."

"What does that have to do with my marrying Casey?"

"It has everything to do with it. Oh, Michael, please listen to me. And believe that I do have your best interests at heart. You and that girl should not marry."

"Why not?"

"I told you. She's not your kind. It would never work."

He shook his head. "Sorry, Mother. That's not good enough."

"Michael . . . you and Casey Cantrell must *not* marry."

His temper blew. "We are going to marry! I realize you look down on her, but that doesn't matter a damn to me."

"It's more than that."

"Then what is it exactly?" Suddenly understanding dawned. "Is it true that her mother was involved with Father? Is that why you object to her—because you're jealous?"

Emily sighed heavily. Then she stood up and faced Michael for a long moment. "We'll talk about this again, later."

As she walked out, Michael felt anger and frustration war within him. Why had Casey gone to see his mother? If she'd just stayed out of her way . . . But he knew he was being unfair. Casey and his mother would have met sometime. And his mother would have reacted just as negatively then as now.

What really bothered him was the sneaking suspicion that Casey was right. The past *was* affecting the present. It was easy to say "The moment is all that matters." But it was becoming harder to believe it.

It was time, he decided, to get to the bottom of this once and for all. Leaving his work on his desk, Michael strode out to his car and drove into London, to his father's office.

Chapter Eleven

*M*ichael strode into the Bredon Enterprises office with barely a glance at the receptionist.

"Why, Mr. Bredon, good afternoon. Your father's . . ."

Ignoring her, he entered his father's private office, closing the door sharply behind him.

Richard glanced up in surprise. He was talking on the telephone. Seeing the determined look on Michael's face, he spoke into the receiver, "Sorry, Charles, something's come up. May I call you back?" After a brief pause he finished, "Good," then hung up.

Michael stood in front of Richard's desk.

"Will you sit down or do you prefer to simply stand there and glare at me?"

Realizing he was being more than slightly ridiculous, Michael sat down. "Sorry. But I just had one hell of a row with Mother."

"You saw your mother?"

"Yes. She came out to the farm."

"Why on earth did she do that?"

"She wanted to talk to me about Casey. Casey went to see her about this business concerning her mother. . . ."

"What?"

"Yes, I'm afraid so."

"She had no business doing that."

"She feels very strongly about this. If you'd simply accepted that letter, she would probably have let it all drop."

"Damn it, Michael, we've been over this! I don't want to discuss it further."

Michael had never heard his father sound so angry. His father's temperament had always been remarkably placid and equable, almost emotionless much of the time. Even when his parents were still living together, unhappily, his father hadn't fought with his mother. He'd simply been excruciatingly polite and reserved. Only the haunted look in his eyes had revealed the depth of his marital unhappiness.

Now Michael said slowly, "I respect your right to privacy. I wouldn't ask about this if it weren't so important. You don't understand. Casey believes there's a shadow from the past hanging over us. She's convinced it will color everything until it's resolved."

Richard gave him a surprisingly gentle look. "*You* don't understand, Michael."

"Perhaps if you'd tell me the truth, I *could* understand."

Richard was silent for a long moment. It was apparent from the drawn expression on his face that he was undergoing some inner turmoil. Finally he

said, "All right. Perhaps if I can make you understand what happened with Jesse Cantrell, you'll
accept that she was no good. And stop trying to
persuade me to read that damn letter."

Michael leaned forward on the chair. "What happened?"

Richard looked past him. There was a distant look
in his eyes as he let his memory drift back to the
past. "It was late winter in 1944. Jesse and your
mother shared a flat. Jesse sang with a USO troupe
at the Montfort Theatre."

His mouth curved in a shadow of a smile. "It used
to be right here, where this office building is now.
They tore it down after the war. I used to come and
watch Jesse perform. God, she was beautiful! I'd
never known anyone like her. I knew from the start
that it wasn't just another wartime romance."

His expression clouded with a pain that even time
couldn't dull. "At least, for me it wasn't just another
romance. I suppose it was after I was shot down over
the Channel that I decided to ask her to marry
me. . . ."

It was the end of March. Officially it was early
spring, but the weather still smacked of winter. It
was cold and rainy and only a very few especially
hardy flowers had dared to bloom in Half-Moon
Square. Richard stood under a spreading plane tree,
watching the stage door exit. He'd been waiting for
over half an hour and was growing impatient. Jesse
should have been out by now. Her matinee performance had ended twenty minutes earlier.

Just as he was thinking about trying to bluff his
way past the watchman at the door, he saw it open.
Jesse came out, wearing the old, worn trench coat

that was so familiar by now. Immediately she glanced at the square. It warmed Richard's heart to see that her first thought was to look for him.

Usually she walked briskly across the street to the square. Today, however, she moved slowly, almost reluctantly. Something's wrong, Richard thought.

When she reached him she didn't smile. "Hi."

"Hi, yourself."

When she didn't move closer, he reached out to take her in his arms. She trembled as he held her. "What's wrong, sweetheart?"

Her voice was muffled against his jacket. "Nothing."

He kissed the top of her head. Without saying another word, he led her to the pub across the square. When they were safely installed at a quiet corner table and had ordered coffee and tea, he asked again, "What's wrong?"

"I told you. Nothing."

Putting his index finger under her chin, he tilted it up so that she looked at him. "Jesse, it's *me*, Richard. Remember?"

There were tears in her eyes.

"Oh, sweetheart, what's wrong?"

She shook her head. "It's nothing, really."

"It's something. You're crying. Jesse, I want to help."

"It's nothing to do with me, Richard. It has to do with someone else."

"Then why are you upset?"

"I'm not upset!" She stopped, then flashed an ironic smile as she wiped the tears from her eyes. "I guess I *am* upset."

"Tell me about it."

She sighed. "Oh, it's just that Betty, one of the girls in the troupe, has a problem. We share a dressing room, so we've become close, and she confided in me."

"Well, what's her problem?"

Her gaze was direct. "What's the usual problem for a young, pretty woman?"

"She's . . . in trouble."

"That euphemistic phrase says it all, doesn't it? How much more trouble can you have than to be pregnant without the benefit of a husband?"

"Who's the father?"

Jesse hesitated. When she answered, she didn't quite meet his look. "An English soldier."

Richard understood now. "I see." Trying hard to keep the conversation on an objective level, he asked, "Is there a possibility he'll marry her?"

"Betty thought so. He told her he loved her. But when she told him last night that she's pregnant, he . . . well, he questioned whether or not she could be sure it's his child. When she assured him it was, he told her he's already married." She finished bitterly, "With three children."

Richard leaned back in his chair. It wasn't the first story like this he'd heard. And he knew it wouldn't be the last.

"I'm sorry."

"You're sorry, I'm sorry. Maybe even the guy is sorry. But that doesn't help Betty."

"What will happen to her?"

Jesse shook her head helplessly. "I don't know. She has family back in the States, but she isn't sure how they'll take this."

"Will she go home now?"

Jesse looked at him directly, her golden-brown eyes poignant. "We're all due to go back in two weeks."

"Two weeks."

"I told you that some time ago."

"Yes. I suppose I forgot." He looked at her, taking in the unhappy downturn of her mouth and the desperately sad expression in those lovely eyes. Finally he took her hands in his and whispered, "I'm not married. I don't have three children. And when I say I love you, I mean it."

Tears stole down her cheeks. "Oh, Richard, the whole time I was listening to Betty, I kept thinking it could be *me* in her place. What is it they say? 'There but for the grace of God go I.'"

"Listen to me, sweetheart. It could *never* be you. I love you, Jesse. Oh, God, how I love you." He sounded fierce, almost angry.

Looking at him, Jesse choked back her tears. "Oh, Richard, I love you so much it scares me. I think of Frank and I feel guilty that I could fall in love again so soon after losing him. I tell myself I should stop seeing you. We come from different worlds, there's no way it could work out. But all my careful arguments disappear when I walk out that stage door and immediately look toward the square to see if you're waiting there."

"I'll always be waiting there, Jesse. I promise you that. Promise me you'll always come to me."

Her voice was a hoarse whisper. "I'll always come to you, Richard."

They looked at each other for an endless moment. Both were silent. It was apparent that neither was interested in the tea or coffee.

"Let's go," Richard said gruffly, throwing down some change on the table.

Outside, it had begun to rain again. He hadn't been able to get a jeep, but he had found a friend with a flat that was going to be empty that day. As they made their way there, neither spoke.

The flat was small and dreary, just one room and a tiny kitchenette. Two small windows that needed a good cleaning let in only a minimal amount of light. This was the first time Richard had been forced to rely on a strange place for their rendezvous. Normally, he got a jeep and they went to the inn, which was beginning to seem almost like home. Other times they went to Jesse's flat when Emily was going to be at work or out of town. But today those two options weren't available.

Now, looking around the strange, dingy flat, Richard felt revulsion well up within him. Jesse deserved better than this.

"Let's get out of here," he muttered angrily.

Taking her arm, he led her outside. They went back to her flat and he said good-bye to her at the door.

"Richard, I'm sorry. . . ."

"You don't have anything to be sorry for. I do, for not being able to give you more."

"Oh, Richard, you've no idea how much you give me. It's enough. More than enough. At least come in and have some tea."

"No, I've got to get back to the base. I only had a short time anyway."

"You're flying tonight?"

He nodded.

Putting her arms around his neck, she looked up

into his slate-blue eyes. "Remember your promise
. . . you won't die."

He smiled grimly. "I won't die, Jesse."

He bent to kiss her once, tenderly. Then he turned
and walked away.

An hour later he was back at the base. He
struggled with the tubes, clasps and straps of his
flying suit, then pulled on three pairs of socks and
thrust his feet into fleece-lined boots.

A few minutes later he was in C flight crew room
for the briefing. About forty young men in flying
suits slouched on hard chairs in the dim room,
listening attentively to the wing commander. He
talked about primary and secondary targets inside
Germany, gesturing with a long pointer on a grainy
aerial picture blown up on a large screen.

Then the opposition map flashed on the screen. It
was marked with red and orange symbols indicating
antiaircraft positions and searchlights.

Richard listened to the dull voice drone on. He'd
heard it a hundred times before. Though he paid
attention, part of his mind was on Jesse. As long as
he lived, he would never forget the way she had
looked as she'd recounted her friend's unhappy
story: "There but for the grace of God go I."

Suddenly the lights came on in the room, and
Richard blinked.

The wing commander finished, "All right, chaps,
that's all. The Jerrys will be on the alert after their
recent heavy bombing of London. They know we'll
retaliate. So look alive. And work fast. The flak will
be heavy."

With the rest of his bomber crew, Richard went to
a row of lockers and took out a parachute, clipping it
to his chest. Then he took out some maps. After

studying them for a few minutes, he tucked them into a canvas pouch, then had a last word with the six men of his crew.

"Ruddy hard mission," the wireless operator commented in a thick Cockney accent.

The rear gunner smiled mischievously. "Ah, come off it, mate. You say that about every one."

The front gunner replied sourly, "That's because every one's a ruddy hard mission."

They went out to the plane. Far down the field, one plane after another coughed into life. Richard's plane trundled down the runway and flew out over the North Sea.

In the cold, rattling plane, Richard thought about Jesse and his promise to her: "I won't die."

They passed the coastal fortifications with only mild flak. Maybe, Richard prayed, this mission will be easy.

But it wasn't, of course. As soon as they entered German territory and neared the targets, what the crew wryly referred to as "fireworks" went off all around them. Searchlights turned the night sky into day. Antiaircraft fire exploded around them, rocking the plane. At the controls, Richard grimly steered the plane into the beautiful, terrifying display.

Suddenly several searchlights caught the plane and remained transfixed on it. Blue radiance shone through the windows. Richard maneuvered the plane to evade the lights, but they followed stubbornly as it lurched, dived and sideslipped.

He found the primary target, dropped the bombs, then turned and headed for home. Everyone cheered with incredible relief. The worst was over. Now all they had to do was get home.

A mass of orange and red pinpoints of light came

soaring up toward the plane, then burst around it, exploding loudly. Richard felt a hard thump and knew they'd been hit. The reassuring drone of the motor changed abruptly and ice-cold air whistled into the plane.

The plane shuddered, then turned into a steep dive. Using all his presence of mind, and sheer physical strength, Richard managed to straighten it out. The stricken plane headed west, lurching back toward England. The port engine was hit, but so far it was still pulling.

"Bloody way to make a living," the copilot joked nervously, his face as white as a sheet.

"We'll go home to tea now," Richard answered, amazed at how calm his own voice sounded. Inside he was terrified.

"Well, if that engine goes, we won't make it. How's your French, Lieutenant?"

Richard managed a smile.

They made it to the Channel before the engine went.

Through the intercom, Richard ordered the men to bail out. When they were all gone, he went, too. As he floated down through the gray dawn into the icy Atlantic, he thought about Jesse. In those few seconds, time itself seemed to stop and everything became crystal clear. What mattered and what didn't. What he needed for his life to be worth living.

If by some miracle I come out of this, he decided as he hit the water, I'm going to marry her as soon as possible.

In the water he unhooked his parachute, then floated through the mildly choppy water. He couldn't see any of his crew, though he thought he heard one of them shout. The water was bone-chilling cold and he knew he couldn't stand it for long. He prayed for a rescue boat.

But when he heard an outboard motor whirring toward him, he suddenly panicked. What if it was the Germans looking for their own downed pilots?

A voice rang out in the distance. "Who are you—Jerry or one of ours?"

Richard laughed, then choked on seawater. He finally managed to cry back, "Stupid bastards, pull me out!"

A boat immediately pulled up alongside of him and strong arms reached out to lift him aboard. "The minute we heard you swear, mate, we knew you was from the RAF. . . ."

Michael looked at his father and waited for him to continue. When he remained silent, he asked quietly, "Did you ask her to marry you?"

Still looking past him, Richard answered, "I bought a ring. A wide gold band with intricate scrollwork. I thought Jesse would like it. And when I got my next extended leave, I went into London. I waited at Half-Moon Square."

He stopped and Michael prompted, "What happened?"

Finally Richard looked at him. "She didn't come. The theater was dark, closed up by then. So I knew she wasn't there. I went to her flat. Your mother told me she'd left that day to return to the States."

"She didn't say good-bye?"

Richard shook his head.

"Or leave a note? Or anything?"

"Nothing."

Michael was silent, deep in thought.

Richard went on in a tired voice, "Your mother told me that her husband had turned up alive after all. I suppose I was just someone to fill the time with while she was waiting for him."

"But if she believed he was dead . . ."

"I don't think she did. I think she just said that to make it more convenient to have an affair."

"Perhaps you're judging her too harshly."

"Then why didn't she see me, explain things? At least leave a letter?" He shook his head. "She didn't even bother to say good-bye."

Michael didn't know what to say. For the first time he understood the unhappiness he'd always sensed in his father. And he understood why his father had so adamantly refused to read Jesse Cantrell's letter. But even if Jesse had used him and then abandoned him, that had nothing to do with Casey. Casey wasn't her mother and shouldn't be made to pay for her sins.

"I appreciate your feelings about Casey now. But you're taking out your bitterness toward her mother on her. It isn't fair."

"I want nothing to do with her, Michael. And after today I never want to discuss Jesse Cantrell again."

"There's something I have to tell you, Father. This isn't a good time, but I suspect no time would be good."

Richard looked at him sharply. "What are you trying to say?"

Michael steeled himself for what he knew would come. "I've asked Casey to marry me."

"What?"

"She hasn't accepted. She wanted to clear up this

business of you and her mother. But now that I know the truth, I intend to do everything I can to persuade her to marry me as soon as possible."

"Michael, she's no good!"

"Perhaps her mother was no good, but that has nothing to do with Casey. Don't you see? As you said before, what happened between you and Jesse Cantrell was a very long time ago. It's time to let go of the past and get on with the present. I don't intend to let what happened in the past ruin my chance of happiness with Casey."

"Knowing how I feel about her, you would still marry her?"

"Please understand. I'm sorry about what happened with you and Jesse. But that has nothing to do with Casey and me. And for your own sake, as well as ours, it's time to let go of your bitterness about the past."

Richard looked at him coldly. "I'll never accept that young woman. Never."

Watching him, Michael knew it was hopeless: his father meant what he said. Without saying another word, he rose and left the room.

At his flat he found Casey sitting by the huge round window in the sitting room. When he came in she stood up and waited for him to cross the room. Her face was pale and drawn and she played nervously with a button on her sweater.

"Michael! I wasn't expecting you so early."

Crossing the room in long strides, he took her in his arms and held her for a moment. Her trembling told him how upset she was. He held her tightly until her trembling stilled. Then, looking down at her, he whispered, "I love you, Casey."

"Oh, Michael, there's something I must tell you."

"It's all right, sweetheart, I know all about it. You saw my mother."

"How did you know?"

"She came to see me."

"She objects to us being involved at least as much as your father does."

"I know. But it doesn't matter." When she glanced away he said, "Look at me, Casey. It *doesn't* matter. They're both caught up in something that was over and done with a long time ago. If they want to hold on to that kind of bitterness, they can. But I won't let it destroy what you and I have."

Looking into his eyes, she felt a rush of love for him. She raised her lips to his in a kiss so tender and sweet she felt as if her heart would melt with happiness. But as the kiss ended and she opened her eyes, she realized there was a hard reality to face.

"Michael, if both your parents strongly object to this marriage, it will make things very difficult for you. I don't want to come between you and them."

"As far as my mother's concerned, you're not coming between us. She never cared for me. I faced that unpleasant fact a long time ago."

"But why? How could she not love her own child?"

Though Michael's tone was determinedly offhand, there was a profound pain in his eyes. Now Casey understood the unhappiness that lay just beneath the surface humor and reckless passion.

"When I was small, there was an old woman who lived with us at the hall. Nanny Wilcox was her name. She'd been my mother's nanny when she was a baby and stayed on to act as a sort of maid-companion when my mother grew up. She was my nanny when I was born. She was the traditional type of old family retainer that you don't see anymore, and was completely devoted to my mother. In fact, my mother still goes to see her regularly."

"She's still alive?"

"Yes. She's in her nineties and her mind's pretty well gone, but she's alive. My mother supports her in a very expensive nursing home near her house in Belgravia. Anyway, when I was a teenager, her mind started to go and she rambled a lot. One day she said something about my birthday being three months earlier than it actually was. My mother was there and she hustled her out of the room. But it made me think."

"You mean that your parents married because your mother was pregnant with you?"

He nodded. "It makes sense. It might explain her feeling resentful toward me. It would also explain the unhappiness of their marriage." His smile was without humor. "Forced marriages often aren't blissful."

"But if, as you say, her mind was already beginning to wander then, you could be reading too much into her remark."

"I don't think so. You see, I was born under rather suspicious circumstances. My mother was up in Scotland, at her family's shooting lodge in the Highlands, when I was born. The only person with her was Nanny Wilcox. They said I was born prematurely and they stayed up there for a couple of months until I was strong enough to travel."

Casey didn't know what to say. It *was* suspicious.

Finally she murmured, "We can't seem to escape the past, can we? You know, all afternoon I've been thinking about my mother's letter, wondering if I should just go ahead and read it. I can't go on not knowing what happened."

"Casey—my father told me what happened between him and your mother."

She was stunned. "He did? When?"

"A little while ago. After talking to my mother, I went to see him. I understand why my mother would object to you. She must have known that my father never really loved her. He was in love with your mother."

Casey felt as if a terrible weight had been lifted from her. At least now she knew the truth; she wouldn't be tormented by questions that no one would answer. She could appreciate Rose's reticence on the subject. Rose clearly hadn't wanted to tell Casey that her mother had been involved in an extramarital affair.

She glanced up at Michael. To her surprise, he looked away. There was something more, she realized. Something he didn't want to discuss.

"Michael, what is it?"

"I told you. Your mother and my father were involved. Now that you know that for certain, you can put it behind you and we can get on with our life together."

"No. There's something more you're not telling me. What is it?"

"I don't know what you mean."

"You're as bad a liar as I am, Michael. Please— you may as well tell me the whole truth. It can't be any worse than what I've already learned—that my mother was unfaithful to my father at a time when he was risking his life fighting for his country."

Michael hesitated, then sighed heavily. "All right.

Let's get it all out, then never discuss it again. It will finally be over."

"That's what I want, too. To put this behind me."

"Let's sit down." As they sat down on the sofa, he put his arm around her.

He's trying to protect me from what's coming, Casey thought. But he can't.

"My father met your mother when she was singing with a USO troupe over here. They became involved and he fell rather hard for her. He intended to ask her to marry him."

"But she was married already."

"Apparently she lied about that, said he was missing in action and presumed dead." There was no way to soften the hard words or the even harder ones to come. Michael went on quickly, anxious to finish this once and for all. "She left abruptly, before he could propose. Apparently your father had shown up. At any rate, she didn't say good-bye to my father, didn't leave a letter for him. Didn't explain in any way. Naturally he felt . . ."

Michael stopped, unsure how to continue.

After a stunned silence, Casey finished for him, "Naturally he thought she'd just been amusing herself with him while my father was away. After all, as you said, it wouldn't be the first time that happened, especially during a war."

Her voice was heartbreakingly matter-of-fact. She was trying with all her might to sound blasé about this, but she couldn't quite bring it off. Her image of her mother had just been completely shattered.

"Oh, sweetheart." Michael hugged her tightly.

"I'm all right," she whispered.

Then the tears began to fall.

Chapter Twelve

Casey spent a sleepless night. Michael held her throughout the long, unhappy hours. He made no move to make love to her until the dawn, when Casey pressed against him and whispered urgently, "Love me, Michael. Love me, now."

Their passion was brief and intense. Michael sensed that Casey was trying to physically exorcise some inner demon by giving herself to him in wild abandonment. Somehow he had the awful sensation that she was slipping away from him. In response, he took her with a passion as desperate as her need for him.

Afterward they lay exhausted in each other's arms.

The next morning he wanted to stay with her or at least have her come with him to the farm, but she insisted that she needed some time to herself.

When he hesitated about leaving, she said with a forced smile, "I'll be all right. Honestly. Now leave, and when you get home you can take me out to a wonderful dinner."

He was only slightly reassured by her brittle gaiety, but he wasn't sure that he should argue with her wish to be alone. He left, but his mind was uneasy.

When he was gone, Casey went into the bedroom and took her mother's letter out of her suitcase. Then she brought it into the living room and sat on the sofa, staring at it. She'd had a whole night to think about what Richard Bredon had told Michael. She accepted that he was probably telling the truth, at least as far as he knew it. But the more she considered it, the less willing she was to believe that cold view of her mother.

The woman she had known for twenty-eight years had been loyal and caring. Jesse Cantrell had never consciously hurt anyone, as far as Casey was aware. Casey couldn't envision her having an affair, leading Richard on, then abandoning him without so much as a good-bye. And she couldn't imagine her being disloyal to Casey's father. Rose herself had said, with apparent sincerity, that Jesse was absolutely loyal.

No, there had to be more to it.

She picked up the phone and dialed Rose's number. Perhaps now Rose would be more willing to discuss Jesse and Richard's relationship. But the phone rang on and on without an answer. Rose was out.

Casey was a mass of nerves, anxious to do something but frustrated because there was nothing she could do. Neither Richard nor Emily, she was certain, would talk to her.

Suddenly she had a thought. There was someone

else who'd been around in 1944, someone who might well know the whole truth. If she would—or could— tell it.

Casey tried to remember exactly what Michael had said about Nanny Wilcox. She was in a nursing home in Belgravia, near his mother's home. Surely the nursing home should be easy to find.

Going to the telephone book, Casey looked up nursing homes in the Belgravia area and discovered there were only two. The first one she called had no patient by the name of Wilcox. The second did.

Half an hour later Casey presented herself at the reception desk. She gave the nurse a vague story about being engaged to a man whose old nanny was a patient there. Her fiancé had asked her to introduce herself to the elderly woman, whom he still remembered fondly.

"Why, how thoughtful," the nurse exclaimed, making Casey feel horribly guilty. "You know, to be perfectly honest, miss, most of our patients get very few visitors. It's so nice when someone remembers them."

"Yes," Casey murmured uncomfortably.

The nurse asked another nurse to take Casey to Mrs. Wilcox's room. For a moment Casey was afraid the nurse would insist on remaining in the room with them. But as they entered the small, private room, the nurse merely said cheerfully, "Mrs. Wilcox, you have a visitor today. Isn't that a nice treat?"

Turning to Casey, she said, "I'll leave you two to visit. When you've finished, just push that buzzer and I'll return to show you out."

When she was gone, Casey moved toward the bed where an ancient, withered woman lay quietly. Her wrinkled hands played absently with the edge of the

white blanket that covered her, and her sparse gray
hair was almost entirely covered by a pink cap that
matched her pink nightgown.

"Emily?" she asked, focusing dim eyes on Casey.

"No, Mrs. Wilcox, I'm not Emily."

Casey sat down in a chair next to the bed. Now
that she was here, she had no idea how to proceed.
She wasn't sure how far gone the woman's mind was,
whether she could even remember the events of
forty years ago.

She began slowly, "I'm a friend of Michael."

"Michael?"

If she didn't even remember Michael, there wasn't
much hope, Casey thought forlornly. Still, she went
on, "Yes, Michael Bredon. You remember—Lady
Emily's son."

"Emily doesn't have a son. She can't have children, poor thing. It's so sad when a woman is
barren."

Her voice was drifty and tremulous, but her eyes,
a pale, watery blue in her soft, almost childish face,
were focusing alertly on Casey now.

"But Mrs. Wilcox, Lady Emily *had* a son. Michael. Don't you remember? You were with her in
Scotland when he was born."

"Scotland?" For a moment she seemed confused,
then understanding dawned. "Oh, you mean the
baby she brought back from America." She smiled,
pleased with herself for remembering. "Oh, yes, *that*
baby. He belonged to the other one."

Casey was thoroughly confused and not at all sure
Mrs. Wilcox knew what she was talking about.
"What other one?"

"The one Lord Richard wanted to marry. But he
didn't marry her. He married Emily. And she gave

him a son, didn't she? That was what he wanted. It
didn't matter that it wasn't hers."

Suddenly she stopped talking and her expression
grew fearful. "But don't tell anyone. It's a secret.
The most important secret. Emily says no one's to
know. Ever."

Oh, my God, Casey thought as nausea washed
over her. The meaning of the old woman's words
was almost too terrible to contemplate. It couldn't
be true. It *couldn't*. The woman was senile, she
didn't realize what she was saying.

Yet all the while she tried to deny it, Casey knew
deep inside that it might very well be true. If it was,
it meant that she and Michael had committed a
terrible sin—and could *never* see each other again.

Mrs. Wilcox sighed tiredly and her eyes closed. "I
think I'll take a nap now," she murmured before
dropping off to sleep.

Casey pressed the buzzer for the nurse and was
escorted out.

"Did you have a nice visit?" the nurse asked
cheerfully.

Casey murmured a polite response, but her mind
wasn't on the talkative young nurse.

"Poor Mrs. Wilcox hardly ever gets any visitors.
Except Lady Bredon, of course. Such a thoughtful
woman, she comes regularly and brings little treats."

Lady Bredon. Of course.

As Casey left the nursing home she flagged down a
taxi and gave Emily's address. She needed to talk to
her immediately.

This time the maid looked less friendly than
before when she opened the door and found Casey
standing there. "I'm afraid Lady Bredon isn't at
home," she began hurriedly.

It was clear she'd been given orders not to admit Casey.

Casey interrupted firmly, "Tell her I've talked to Nanny Wilcox. I think you'll find she's at home after all."

Looking flustered, the maid left without inviting Casey to step into the entryway. A minute later she returned with a barely concealed look of intense curiosity on her face. "Her Ladyship's at home, miss. This way, please."

She led Casey to the same sitting room as before, then left.

Emily Bredon stood rigidly near the fireplace, the expression on her face an ugly combination of fury and fear. But Casey was no longer in awe of her. She walked up and leveled a direct look at her.

"How dare you question my old servant!"

"It's pointless being angry with me, Lady Bredon. I know the truth. I only came here to confront you with it."

To Casey's surprise, her haughty countenance crumpled. She almost dropped into a nearby chair and buried her face in her hands. Her words were muffled. "For forty years I managed to keep it a secret. It should have remained that way. But you had to come. As soon as I saw you, it was like looking at Jesse again. And I was afraid . . . so afraid. . . ."

Casey had hoped against hope that Mrs. Wilcox was wrong. At the very least, she'd prayed there'd be another, more innocent interpretation to her words. That was really why she'd come here, to give Emily Bredon an opportunity to put to rest the awful suspicion that lay like an icy hand around her heart.

Instead, Emily had confirmed the worst.

It was all Casey could do to remain standing. Her knees had suddenly gone all wobbly.

Pulling herself together, she whispered accusingly, "How could you? How could you take her child?"

Emily shuddered, then leaned back in the chair. Her face was absolutely white and seemed to have aged years in only a moment. Looking past Casey, she said dully, "I knew Jesse was pregnant with Richard's child when she left England to return to the States with her husband. Richard didn't know. Her husband had turned up alive, you see. Badly wounded, but alive. He was brought to a hospital here, then sent back to the States. She went with him. It all happened very quickly. At first Richard was crushed. But after a while I persuaded him it was for the best. Jesse wasn't right for him, I was."

She looked at Casey defiantly. "*I* was. I'd been in love with him all my life. And I knew that eventually he'd realize he loved me. If only Jesse hadn't been there to ruin everything. Who was she but a common little upstart who would never fit in with his people, his way of life?"

Casey had a flash of inspiration. "Did my mother try to say good-bye to him? Perhaps in a letter?"

Emily had the grace to look guilty. Glancing away, she admitted reluctantly, "There was a letter. But I didn't give it to Richard. What good would it have done? She was married, her husband was alive. Richard couldn't have her. So why should he torture himself with longing for her?"

"And so he married you."

"Yes."

"But you couldn't have children."

She shook her head helplessly. "I found out at once. I didn't know what to do. It was so important to Richard. He was the last of his family. The line *must* go on. Without an heir, I was afraid someday he would leave me."

"How did you ever persuade my mother to give up her child?"

"Richard was away on a tour of duty. I wrote to tell him I was pregnant. He was overjoyed. It seemed to make up for the unhappiness he'd felt when Jesse left."

"You lied to him?"

"I *had* to. It was the only way. I told him I was going to stay in Scotland for a while. Instead, I went to the States, to Jesse. Her child was born while I was there. A boy. All I could think of was that it was a son for Richard."

"But it was Jesse's child. Why would she give it up to you?"

"I told her that Richard wanted the child. He could give it everything she and her husband couldn't—wealth, position. And after all, *he* was the father, not the man she was married to."

"My father agreed to this?"

"He was still in hospital. He had slipped into a coma, apparently, and they didn't know if he would ever come out of it. He didn't know Jesse had even borne a child. I pointed out to her that even if her husband survived and got well, he probably wouldn't want another man's child. It would be a very unhappy situation to raise her child in."

"You *pointed out* all these things to her," Casey said harshly. "You mean you badgered her, playing on her fears, on her concern for the welfare of her baby. My God, she'd just gone through childbirth, she was probably in no state to make such a decision!"

"She agreed, finally. She accepted the fact that it would be best for the child to be with his father."

"So you brought Michael back to Scotland and pretended he was your child, born prematurely."

"It was for the best!" Emily insisted. "He's had *everything.*"

"Everything except a mother's love. You denied him that."

Emily didn't respond. Casey stood looking down at her, feeling tremendous anger toward her. So many people had suffered—Michael, his father, Jesse—all because of Emily's blind obsession to have Richard.

Then it occurred to her that for all of Emily's desperate efforts, she hadn't won after all. Richard had never loved her. Casey began to feel pity mixed with her anger. Emily was a pathetic figure, really.

"When you came, it was almost as if Jesse were back," Emily said slowly. "She couldn't have Richard, but you were close to having Michael." Her mouth twisted in bitter irony. "I suppose there was almost a poetic justice in it."

Then, looking at Casey, Emily continued with some semblance of her old control, "You understand now why I told Michael you and he must not marry. He is your half brother."

"I understand," Casey whispered.

Suddenly she could take no more. She turned and ran from the house.

She went back to the flat, packed quickly and left. When she was gone, it occurred to her that she'd left her mother's letter on the table in the sitting room. But it didn't matter now. She knew what was in it.

Casey called Rose once more. There was still no answer. Having no idea where else to go, she checked her suitcases in at a nearby train station, then walked the crowded city streets. Finally, exhausted, she went into a restaurant and had some coffee. When she'd finished, she knew she had to call Michael. It was dark now, nearly five o'clock. He would be back at the flat, wondering what had happened to her. She had to tell him the truth. But she couldn't bring herself to do it in person.

Stepping into a telephone kiosk, she dialed his number.

"Hello."

"Michael . . ."

"Casey, where the hell are you? I've been so worried. I came home and found you gone, along with your things. What's going on?"

"I went to see Nanny Wilcox. I thought she might be able to tell me something about what happened. As it turned out, what she told me was so . . . so important, I felt I had to see your mother again to confirm it."

"Casey, what are you talking about?"

"Oh, Michael, your mother admitted to me that you're not her child."

There was a silence on the other end of the line. The fact that Michael didn't immediately question her statement proved that he sensed it was true.

"That's almost a relief," he finally responded. "At least now I know why she never loved me. But Casey, what does that have to do with you and me?"

"Michael, I don't know how to say this." Her voice had grown shaky. She paused to pull herself together, then went on, "Your mother was Jesse Cantrell."

"What?"

"It's true. She became pregnant when she was

involved with your father. Later, when she'd returned home, Emily went to her. She'd learned that she couldn't have children, so she persuaded Jesse to give you up. She said that Richard wanted his child and could give him much more than Jesse ever could."

"Casey, that's preposterous. It would mean—"

"I know what it means, Michael. My God, I know."

Even through the telephone, it was apparent that he was trying very hard to remain calm. "Casey, listen to me. My mother was lying. She just wants to keep us apart because she's still bitterly jealous of your mother."

"I wish that were true."

"It *is*. Sweetheart, we couldn't feel what we feel for each other if we were brother and sister. I refuse to believe it."

"I believe it, Michael. And because of that we can never see each other again."

"Casey, where are you?"

She didn't answer.

"Are you at Rose Donovan's?"

"No. I must go now."

"Don't hang up! Listen to me. It isn't true. It can't be. I'll talk to both my mother and father. I'll get at the truth."

"Michael, we've finally learned the truth. And it means we can't love each other."

"Casey, I can't lose you now. We have to talk about this. Meet me at my father's office."

"I can't."

"All right, at least meet me outside, in the square. I'll talk to him, then we'll both go together to talk to my mother again."

"Michael, I can't."

"You have to. You can't just run away. Meet me at Half-Moon Square."

"I won't be there, Michael."

"I will be. I'll wait all night if I have to."

She hung up. Only the fact that a woman stood waiting impatiently outside the kiosk kept Casey from bursting into tears. She had no idea where to go, what to do. Then she remembered Rose. Suddenly she needed Rose's loving comfort very badly. Leaving the kiosk to the impatient woman, she hailed a taxi and went to Rose's house.

When Casey hung up, Michael stood staring at the receiver for a moment, as if willing her to come back on the line. Then, swearing furiously, he slammed down the phone. Noticing Jesse's letter on the table, he picked it up and shoved it in his pocket, then left. He would give the letter to his father whether Richard wanted it or not. Then he would wait for Casey. And when she met him at the square—*when*, not *if*—they would get to the bottom of this. They had a lifetime to spend together. A lifetime that wasn't going to be sacrificed on the altar of the tragic past.

Casey was prepared to camp on Rose's doorstep. But as the taxi drew up in front of the townhouse, she saw Rose standing on the threshold, having just unlocked the door.

At the sight of Casey's devastated expression, Rose ushered her into the sitting room, sat her down on the sofa and said, "My poor child, what's happened?"

Casey told her everything—her involvement with

Michael; his parents' opposition; and finally, Emily's admission of the truth.

"Oh, Casey." Rose's voice was full of compassion.

"Rose, it means—"

"I know what it means, child. Listen, there's so much to tell you. I probably should have told you before, but Jesse made me swear that I would keep it secret. However, it's clear that the time for secrets is past. They've already done far too much damage."

"What do you mean?"

"Casey, there's a great deal you need to know. But for the moment, the most important thing is this—you and Michael are *not* related."

"Emily lied?"

"No, she told the truth, as far as she knows it. Casey . . ." Rose hesitated, then went on in a rush, "Damn, there's no easy way to say this, and it's crucial that you know. So I'll simply tell you straight out—you were adopted."

Casey wasn't sure whether to be relieved or depressed. The idea was so totally unexpected. She was completely unprepared for it.

"I'm sorry to have to say it so bluntly, without taking the time to prepare you. But you need to know the truth. I urged your mother to tell you, but she refused."

"Rose, are you sure of this?"

Rose smiled gently. "I understand it's something of a shock. But believe me, I am quite sure. You see, I arranged the adoption. Later I'll show you the papers and tell you more about it. But for now you need to meet with Michael and assure him that everything will be all right between you two."

"Rose, I need to know what happened."

"All right. These are the bare facts. Your mother did have Richard's son. That son was Michael. Emily did persuade her to give up the child. I can only imagine the state of mind Jesse was in at the time. She'd left Richard, whom she truly loved, out of a sense of loyalty to your poor wounded father. She didn't know if your father would live, or if he did, how he would feel about raising another man's son. Casey, she loved Michael desperately. When she gave him up to Richard, it was the greatest sacrifice of her life, greater even than when she left Richard to go with Frank."

"But where do I come in?"

"Your mother wondered why Richard never acknowledged the fact that she'd given him his son. She wrote to him several times, asking for news of Michael, but he never answered the letters. Finally, she came to London in 1955. She'd never been able to have another child, because even though your father lived, he was sterile. She missed Michael terribly and felt that she *had* to see him. She came to me, asking for my help. I interceded with Emily and they met. She discovered that Emily had destroyed her letters to Richard, and that Emily had never told him the truth about Michael."

"Did she tell Richard the truth then?"

"She considered it. But as Emily pointed out so convincingly, what good would it do? It would hurt everyone concerned—Richard and, especially, Michael. He was only ten years old. How could he handle that shocking discovery? It would devastate him to learn he was illegitimate."

"So she left without telling Richard the truth."

"Yes. But she did see Michael. She accomplished

that much, at least. She didn't tell him who she was. Oh, Casey, I was there when they met and it was the most heartbreaking thing I've ever seen. Jesse wanted to take him in her arms and tell him who she was, how much she loved him. But all she could do was look at him and say, 'What a beautiful boy you are.'"

Tears stung Casey's eyes. "My poor mother."

"Yes. Now you know why I admired her so. I wanted to do what I could to help her. At that time I was running an orphanage. There was a baby girl, less than a year old. Her father was an American soldier, her mother an English girl. They'd married after a whirlwind romance and he took her back to his home. But it didn't work out, and the girl eventually returned. She came from a desperately poor family in the East End. She couldn't support her baby, so she gave her up for adoption. I showed Jesse the little girl, who had red hair and brown eyes. Jesse said, 'She looks like me. She might almost be my own.' I told her that the little girl could be her own, if she wished."

Rose paused, looked gently at Casey and finished, "That little girl was *you,* Casey."

"Why didn't she tell me I was adopted?"

"She was afraid one question would lead to another and the truth about Michael would come out."

"Oh, Rose." Casey hugged her tightly and cried the tears she'd held back all day.

"There, there, Casey, it's all right. Everything's all right now. You go to Michael and be happy with him. You two deserve to find the happiness Jesse and Richard lost."

Sitting back, Casey wiped the tears from her eyes.

As Rose had said, there was still a great deal to learn, to accept. But for now, all that mattered was that Michael was waiting for her. And she must go to him.

In his father's office, Michael threw Jesse's letter down on the desk.

"I've already said I don't want to read that," Richard snapped.

"I'm not asking for Casey's sake now, Father. I'm asking for mine. I love her and I want to marry her. Think about how you felt about Jesse, and you'll understand how I feel."

Richard was silent. But it was apparent Michael's words had had the desired effect. He didn't shove the letter away. Instead he said soberly, "I still oppose the match."

"You can oppose it till hell freezes over. But I'm going to marry her."

Turning on his heel, Michael strode out of the room, slamming the door behind him.

Outside, he crossed the street and entered the small park. It was dark now, and it had begun to rain, but streetlights gave out a warm glow. Standing under a tree, Michael pulled up the collar of his coat and waited for Casey. He refused to let himself consider the possibility that she wouldn't come.

In his office, Richard hesitated for just a moment. Then, picking up the letter and slipping it in his pocket, he hurried out to catch Michael.

On the sidewalk in front of the building, he looked around. At first he thought he was too late and Michael had already left. Then he saw him standing in the park across the street. Just as Richard started to cross the street, he saw a hauntingly familiar figure race across the park toward Michael—a young woman in a tan trench coat, her red hair blowing wetly in the rain.

As she flew into Michael's arms, Richard felt an odd sensation of the years slipping away, the past repeating itself. Slowly, he took Jesse's letter from his pocket. After a moment's hesitation, he opened it. Standing there in the light rain, he read:

My Dearest Richard,

It is dawn, the end of a long and sleepless night. I am here, in London again, so close to you and yet so far away. I came to ask you a question. But the question has been answered and I know there is no point in seeing you. Instead, I am writing this letter to tell you the truth. Now isn't the right time for the truth to be known. So I will seal this when I have finished and keep it hidden until I am gone.

I loved you, darling. More than you will ever know. I wrote you a letter, telling you this, before I left London in 1944. But I've just learned that you never received that letter. Here, then, is the truth: Frank wasn't dead, as they had thought. He lived, barely, and was brought to a London hospital. They wanted to fly him back to the States immediately. As his wife I was expected to go with him. It all happened so fast. I tried to call, but you were on a mission. So I left the letter that you never received.

I don't know if I will ever be able to forgive Emily for what she did. But I understand, in a way. She loves you, too.

The important thing you must know is this—I

loved you then. But I was honor-bound to go with Frank. How could I leave him, even though it was you I'd come to love with all my heart?

The other important thing you must know is this—Michael is *our* child. Emily persuaded me to give him up. She said you wanted him. She said it would be in his best interests. I was weak and ill and thought she was right. Now, I wonder. I am his mother and I wish I could have raised him. But there is great comfort in knowing that you have him. I gave him to you, Richard, not because you could give him more than I could, but because he was the one thing I *could* give you when I couldn't give myself.

I have seen Michael and he is everything I knew he would be. Oh, Richard, he is the best of both of us. I know you love him. So do I. But I can't have him, any more than I can have you.

Frank and I cannot have children, but Rose has arranged for me to adopt a little girl. She looks amazingly like me, with red hair and light brown eyes. She can never take Michael's place in my heart, of course. It would be unfair to place such a burden on anyone, especially a child. But she will fill part of the emptiness of my life.

> I love you still.
> Yours forever,
> Jesse

When Richard looked up, his eyes were blurred . . . and not from the rain. Forty years of bitterness had been lifted from him.

She had loved him after all. So much so that she had made the greatest sacrifice for him. Though he'd lost her, in a way she'd come back to him now. For the rest of his life he would have the memory of her love to warm him.

Looking at the square once more, he saw Michael and Casey walking away, his arm around her protectively, her head resting against his shoulder.

Through the blur of Richard's tears in the rain, the past forty years dissolved . . . and it almost seemed as if it were an RAF lieutenant and the girl he loved walking away together from Half-Moon Square. . . .